Anya didn't need him.

Ben thought of those two wardrobes and he found himself grinning. He knew, deep down, that the reaction that had made her cling to him, that had let him grasp her hand, that had forced her to hold it as if it was there to save her, was an aberration.

Anya. One strong woman.

Wardrobes. Two separate beds.

They were now colleagues. There was a whole new future to think about…

Um…think about what? She was still in the midst of shock and grief. *Back away*, he told himself. But even as he did, he was turning back to the bungalow.

Home? Back to Anya?

She'd be in the shower. He could imagine her there. Maybe shaking again as the events of the afternoon replayed in her head?

She was his colleague. He needed to support her.

Yes, he needed to go home.

Dear Reader,

One of the most glorious sights in the world has to be wild dolphins cruising in the open ocean. I'm lucky enough to live by the sea, and the sight of dolphins always seems a blessing. A couple of times, though, there have been strandings, and then it seems the whole community wants to help.

The last time this occurred, I thought what a great way it was to bring people together. And then, turning to my writing, I thought what a great way it was to bring Anya and Ben together.

Strandings take mass effort, with medical care required for not only the dolphins but the volunteers helping to save them. Thus, Drs. Anya and Ben are at the forefront of my rescue, and when the dolphins find their happy ending…well, read and see.

Enjoy!

Marion

HEALED BY THEIR DOLPHIN ISLAND BABY

———

MARION LENNOX

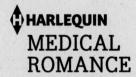

HARLEQUIN

MEDICAL
ROMANCE

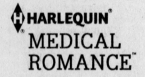

HARLEQUIN®
MEDICAL
ROMANCE™

Recycling programs
for this product may
not exist in your area.

ISBN-13: 978-1-335-73763-2

Healed by Their Dolphin Island Baby

Copyright © 2023 by Marion Lennox

For questions and comments about the quality of this book,
please contact us at CustomerService@Harlequin.com.

Harlequin Enterprises ULC
22 Adelaide St. West, 41st Floor
Toronto, Ontario M5H 4E3, Canada
www.Harlequin.com

Printed in U.S.A.

This book is dedicated to Lorraine, and to
Bill and Mandy and Scott, who were with David
and me on our first ever tropical island escapade.
We had the most glorious time.
Thank you for the most glorious friendship.

Marion Lennox has written over one hundred romance novels and is published in over one hundred countries and thirty languages. Her international awards include the prestigious RITA® Award (twice!) and the *RT Book Reviews* Career Achievement Award for "a body of work which makes us laugh and teaches us about love." Marion adores her family, her kayak, her dog and lying on the beach with a book someone else has written. Heaven!

Books by Marion Lennox

Harlequin Medical Romance

Second Chance with Her Island Doc
Rescued by the Single Dad Doc
Pregnant Midwife on His Doorstep
Mistletoe Kiss with the Heart Doctor
Falling for His Island Nurse
Healing Her Brooding Island Hero
A Rescue Dog to Heal Them
A Family to Save the Doctor's Heart
Dr. Finlay's Courageous Bride

Harlequin Romance

English Lord on Her Doorstep
Cinderella and the Billionaire

Visit the Author Profile page
at Harlequin.com for more titles.

PROLOGUE

'BEN, THIS IS my fiancée, Dr Anya Greer.'

Mathew's chest puffed up with satisfaction. All was well in his world, and he was pleased to let his colleague from university days know it.

'Anya, this is Dr Ben Duncan, who's kindly agreed to act as locum for us during our honeymoon.'

Dr Ben Duncan had had little to do with Dr Mathew Cummins since they'd trained together, but he knew him to be a skilled, if slightly pompous, clinician and he was interested in meeting the woman he was about to marry.

But why did the realisation that Mathew's bride was gorgeous surprise him?

The woman smiling a greeting had, he gathered, just come from performing a minor procedure in Theatre and she was dressed in green hospital scrubs. She was almost a head shorter than him. Her shiny black hair was caught back in a sensible knot but curls were wisping outward. Her skin was warmly honey-coloured, her smile was wide and her eyes twinkled at him as she held out her hand.

'I'm very pleased to meet you.' Her voice was soft and welcoming. 'I hope Merriwood doesn't give you too much trouble while we're away.'

And as he took her hand he was caught by the last thing he'd expected. A stab of…jealousy?

What the…? Where had that come from?

Mathew could keep marriage, he thought, jerking himself back from unwanted sensations, almost in shock. He wanted nothing to do with relationships. The ache in his back, the weakness in his left leg—surely they were enough to remind him of the disaster emotional connections caused. The tragedy of his marriage had been the result of just such instant attraction. A moment's impulse. A lifetime of regret.

Mathew was doing it much better, he told himself. Apparently he'd known Anya since childhood and they'd been friends for ever. This marriage, Mathew had told Ben—and yep, there'd been pomposity in this statement as well—was based on sense and a shared commitment to the good of the town.

Wow. To marry a woman this gorgeous because of sense and a commitment to the town…

Um, stupid thought. No doubt there'd be hot sex in there as well, and years of kids and fun and family.

Meanwhile he'd held Anya's hand for just a bit

too long. He released it and backed away, leaning heavily on his cane.

'Congratulations,' he said, somewhat inanely. 'I wish you both joy.'

'Thank you,' she said, still smiling. But had the twinkle faded a little as she glanced at Mathew? 'I'm sure we'll have it. In spades.'

Joy.

Anya had finished work for the day—well, for three weeks, until she and Mathew returned from their honeymoon. The staff had waved her off with excitement. When she reached the car park someone had wrapped her little sedan in streamers and tied tin cans to the back. She considered removing them, but then decided people would love seeing her car tootle through the town wrapped like this, jangling loudly enough to bring them all out to see.

The town would love this.

Wasn't that what this was all about?

No, she told herself firmly. It was about a wedding. Joy. She and Mathew, for ever and ever.

So why, as she drove home, was she thinking of a tall, lean, dark-eyed guy leaning heavily on a cane, smiling at her with warmth, holding her hand as he'd smiled? She could still almost feel that hold.

Was this last moment panic, a stupid, fleeting thought that there were more men out there? Other men than Mathew?

Oh, get a grip. She turned the corner of her street and her mum was out on the lawn waiting for her. Someone must have warned her that her daughter would be driving home in style. Neighbours were out, too, laughing and cheering as she emerged from her decorated car.

Everyone was so happy about this wedding.

And so was she, she told herself.

Joy. It was there for the asking. A happy ever after with Mathew.

The feel of a strange doctor's hand in hers...

That was last-minute nerves, she told herself. Forget it. She had a wedding to prepare for.

And back at the hospital...

'Come out with us tonight,' Mathew urged Ben. 'It won't be a wild buck's night, just Dad and my uncles and a couple of mates I can depend on not to try and get me drunk.' He glanced at Ben's cane. 'I figure you're the same. If you're still on painkillers you won't be drinking.'

'I'm not,' Ben said shortly. 'But thanks, no.'

'Oh, I understand,' Mathew said, suddenly contrite. 'It's only been twelve months since you lost Rihanna. You'll hardly be wanting to think about weddings. You go to bed, mate. Your apartment kitchen has the basics, but I can ask

Beth, our hospital cook, to send something more substantial.'

'I'm okay.' Ben's face tightened. 'I can look after myself.'

'Yeah, but…you know you only have to ask. One thing I've prided myself on, the staff here are trained to be kind. Anything you need…'

'Thanks, but no,' Ben said, and managed to swallow the rest of his thoughts.

Anything he needed?

He did *not* need kindness.

CHAPTER ONE

'IT'S TIME TO GO, sweetheart.'

Twenty-four hours later it was, indeed, time to go. Anya took one last look at the reflection in her mirror, and it was all she could do not to grimace.

This wasn't her. Her dress was a mass of white satin, with a glittering overlay of silver toile. Her curls had been skilfully arranged to cascade from a central silver tiara, loaned by her future mother-in-law, and the cosmetics applied by the local beautician—free of charge—were making her face feel—and look—as if it might crack at any minute.

The whole image made her feel like a picture in a birthday cake book she'd been shown before her seventh birthday.

'Choose a cake, sweetheart,' her mother had told her. *'You can have any cake you like, but Mrs Olsen says she's aching to make Ballroom Beauty.'*

Mrs Olsen was the lady who'd organised discreet drop-offs of secondhand clothes whenever they were needed. Anya had longed for the fire engine cake in the 'For Boys' section' of the book, but even at seven she'd known her duty. Her birthday cake had therefore been a gorgeous sugary version of Ballroom Beauty, complete with plastic doll's head sticking out the top.

And Anya had been…grateful.

Life, for Anya, had been a long exercise in being grateful. She'd wanted to join the Sea Scouts, but 'Mrs Grayson says you can join her ballet class for free and it's on the same night'. She'd ached for a puppy for her twelfth birthday, but Mayor Cummins and his son Mathew had turned up a week before, bearing a kitten. 'Our Tabby's had a litter of six, and we knew your littlie wanted a pet.'

Anya's mother, Reyna, had been an 'outsider', a bride from the Philippines. Mike Greer, Australian tourist, had meet her when she was halfway through her university course, and their unplanned pregnancy had seen Mike bring a shocked, disoriented bride back to Merriwood. Reyna had been madly in love, but she'd known no one and she'd spoken little English.

The community, however, had rallied to the cause, and when Mike went back to his job as a long-distance truck driver the town had embraced her. When Mike had died in a fiery highway crash, leaving a financially destitute wife and small daughter, that support had magnified tenfold.

Anya had thus been raised to be unendingly grateful. Even her medical degree was cause for gratitude. She'd had the marks, she'd won a scholarship, but her mother's distress at Anya's need to study in Sydney meant that she'd still needed support.

Once again, the town had rallied, assuring Reyna they'd be there for her. Her teachers had assured Reyna that university holidays were long, that Anya would sail through medicine and be home in no time. She could come home, practice medicine in Merriwood and live happily ever after. Plus that nice boy Mathew Cummins—son of the kitten-giver—had left town to study medicine three years before and he'd look out for her.

He had, indeed, looked out for her.

Mathew had been super-kind, Anya conceded. He'd made that first frightening year as a cash-strapped country kid into a success.

She'd loved medicine, and when Mathew invited her to come home to Merriwood to join him at Merriwood Hospital, when her mother, when Mathew's parents, when practically every person in Merriwood had assumed both Mathew and Anya would practice medicine together here— well, why not?

Plus her mother's health was failing. A type

one diabetic since childhood, Reyna's one pregnancy had almost been a disaster, and long-term complications meant she was coping with dialysis three times a week. A kidney transplant had failed and she now also had heart issues. The community was caring for her, however, as they'd always cared for her, and Anya was endlessly grateful.

So why not agree? Come home and be a doctor in Merriwood? Yes, she would.

And she'd marry Mathew.

It was funny how she'd never split those options in her head, though. It was only now, staring at the billowing folds of the gown the town's sewing bee had made for her, that she was thinking suddenly, stupidly—sadly?—of that fire engine cake. Of the load of obligations she owed Mathew.

And weirdly...still of that handshake. A doctor called Ben?

Um...no. Ridiculous.

'Sweetheart, you can be ten minutes late but no more.' Her mother's arm was around her waist. She was beaming into the mirror. For her mum this was a dream come true. 'Let's go.'

Her mother deserved this day, Anya thought, and mentally squared her shoulders. Right, let's get this over with.

And then she wondered if a bride should be

thinking such thoughts on her wedding day. And why was she thinking them now?

It wasn't as if she didn't want to marry Mathew. He was a nice man, endlessly kind. He was a great country doctor. They'd set up the best practice and her mum would be so proud.

So would the whole town.

This wedding itself was yet another act of kindness. Mathew's sister had done the flowers—and wow, Anya's bouquet was gorgeous. His mum's friends were decorating the church and hall, and Mathew's best friend from school, Jeanie Ray, was doing the catering.

That was a bit of a risk, though, Anya thought. Jeanie had just opened her own catering business and Anya wasn't too sure of her capabilities. With Mathew's parents inviting almost the whole town to a pre-wedding lunch, with the reception to follow, the catering needs were huge.

'But it's such a great opportunity,' Mathew had told her, reproachful that she should question his decision. 'It'll launch her business like nothing else can, and she's giving us a cut rate. We should be grateful.'

How many times had Anya heard that line? It had been all she could do not to wince.

And Anna had thought…if you weren't marrying the charity kid, would you want your inexperienced friend to do the catering?

But Anya *was* the charity kid, and she couldn't argue.

That was what this wedding was all about, Anya decided as she saw trouble in her mother's face and gave her a reassuring hug. Somehow it seemed a thank you for this whole community, and Mathew was a part of it. He loved her—she knew he did—but she'd long ago realised there was a part of him that revelled in do-gooding.

Well, so what? It was good to be marrying someone who was kind, and the thought of not marrying him…the reproach that'd follow…her mother's devastation…

For heaven's sake, what was she thinking? She took a deep breath, steadied and smiled down into her mother's face. And then she hesitated. Reyna looked…pale? Washed out?

'Mum, are you okay?'

Reyna glanced into the mirror and winced. 'I'm okay,' she assured her daughter. 'My tummy has butterflies, but why wouldn't it? My only daughter, marrying. I'm so proud. But I shouldn't have agreed to let Myra Stevens do my make-up. She's made me look pale.'

Hmm. The doctor in Anya looked a little longer at her mum, thinking, yes, she was wearing unaccustomed make-up, but her eyes seemed shadowed and a bit too big for her face. But then, her mum had been so nervous about today. So happy.

As she was. She was marrying Mathew. She was heading for happy ever after.

Do it!

'Okay, Mum, let's go.'

'You know I want grandbabies,' Reyna said as they settled into the limousine Mathew's dad had organised. 'Do you think you might start trying straight away?'

'Straight away!'

'Well, you know, my kidneys,' her mum said diffidently, fussing over the arrangement of her daughter's Cinderella-type gown. There was even a hoop under it! 'Oh, Anya, you're making me so happy.'

But Anya's attention was caught. 'What about your kidneys? Everything's stable, isn't it? That visit to the specialist while I was away… You told me everything was fine. Mum…'

'I *am* fine,' her mother said resolutely. 'Everything's fine. Everything's wonderful. Now, let's go get you married!'

Ben was having a lazy Saturday afternoon—and he wasn't enjoying it one bit.

Merriwood's hospital was in a very nice setting. Some might even say gorgeous. Nestled in a valley overlooking the New South Wales south coast, he was looking down through bushland to the long stretch of beach and the sapphire glint of the ocean in the distance. From the grounds of the church along the headland he could hear music—Pachelbel's *Canon*? The music was mixing with the birdsong in the eucalypts overhead. The day was perfect. It was a great day for a wedding.

In the hospital behind him were sixteen not very sick patients, and Ben had nothing to do.

Ben was second on call and he was feeling useless. 'I can't have a honeymoon without you, mate,' Mathew had pleaded. 'Anya's a doctor too. That means instead of three doctors, Merriwood will only have one, and Mary's elderly. She won't be able to cope.'

But it had turned out Dr Mary Carmichael was a mere sixty, fighting fit and aching to have the hospital to herself. She'd also bristled when Ben had arrived and been introduced.

'I can manage alone here, and Mathew's organised the doctors in the next town to do the routine clinics. Unless there's an emergency, I have no idea how you'll make yourself useful. What was Mathew thinking?'

She'd reluctantly let him check on two of the nursing home patients this morning, and at lunchtime she'd handed him an application for funding for a new CT scanner to fill out. 'If you must work then you can do this.'

The paperwork for the application was sitting beside him. He'd looked at it, but he had no idea of the financial or practical requirements of this hospital.

He should leave. Mathew had persuaded him to come to be kind, and he should have known. He'd endured over a year of unending kindness. Enough!

The sounds of the distant music faded and Ben thought, *They'll be making their vows now.* That took him back to a place he didn't want to go. A cathedral in central Sydney, with a crowd of Sydney's fashionable set in attendance. Rihanna, a television presenter, had looked almost ethereal as she'd made vows that, in retrospect, she'd had no intention of keeping.

They'd only been dating for four months when she'd told him she was pregnant, and her devastation had seemed overwhelming. She'd said her career, even her life, would be over if they didn't marry. He'd believed her. He'd also believed her, two weeks after the wedding, when she told him she'd miscarried. It was only later that the doubts had edged their way in. Ben's parents were old money with links to British aristocracy. They'd represented something Rihanna wanted.

And she'd wanted it right to the moment their car had smashed at speed, killing her instantly.

It had taken a while to regain his memory, but he now had flashbacks to their last night together. There'd been a society dinner. He'd arrived late after a hospital emergency, to find

Rihanna in a secluded alcove with one of her colleagues. He'd seen the intimate body language, the guilty start when he'd approached. Suspicions had turned to certainty, and on the way home he'd finally confronted her.

Her anger had blown him away. She was no longer the vivacious society beauty he'd fallen for, but a woman vituperative in her anger.

'Yes, I'm having an affair, but what do you expect? All you ever do is work. Derek knows how to have a good time.'

'Then go to Derek,' he'd said heavily. 'And slow down.' He'd gone to the function in a taxi, straight from the hospital, and she was driving him home. It was raining, the roads were slippery and she was well over the speed limit. 'Rihanna...'

'What do you mean, go to Derek?' she'd snapped, and her foot had firmed on the accelerator.

'I want a divorce.'

'You can't divorce me,' she'd said in a high-pitched voice that had him suddenly wondering how much she'd been drinking before he'd joined her. 'Because guess what? I'm pregnant again. I'm carrying the Duncan family heir. Your mummy and daddy will be so pleased...'

And then oncoming lights, a screech of brakes...and nothing until he'd woken what turned out to be weeks later, to see his mother standing over him. And crying.

'Ben, I'm so sorry. Your back…you've crushed two vertebrae. They're doing their best but they're not sure you're going to be able to walk again.'

'Rihanna?' He remembered struggling to get the word out.

'She's dead. Oh, Ben…'

What followed then had been surgeries, more surgeries, pain, months of intense rehabilitation.

Somewhere in there he'd been faced with the coroner's report on Rihanna. Alcohol. Drugs.

But this time she had been speaking the truth. She'd been weeks pregnant, but he didn't want to know who to.

Block it out. It didn't matter. There was only months of pain—and kindness, kindness and more kindness.

He'd kept up with his medical skills. He'd used the time to read, study, listen in on online conferences, determined to get his life back.

And through it all he'd endured the unending sympathy of family and friends.

That sounded ungrateful, but by now he'd had kindness and sympathy up to his ears. He was still walking with a cane, his back still ached, but it was time to get his life back. Returning to hands-on medicine was to have been the final step back into work, and when Mathew had come to see him he'd thought this could be step one.

'A three-week locum, mate, you'll be doing me a huge favour.' Great. He'd do this, and then a couple more before returning to full-time work.

But now here he was, sitting in the sun, realising that Mathew would have been able to get a hundred locums to work in this place and knowing also that Mary could well cope without him. What was the town doing with three doctors anyway? Why had Mathew even employed Anya, when surely Mary and Mathew could have coped? More kindness?

One of the nurses had told him Anya's background—the daughter of a widow, a life of poverty and need. 'It's so lovely that Mathew's marrying her. Her mum wants her at home so much, and he's so kind.'

And that was causing another niggle. As students he'd grown to know Mathew well—with surnames starting with C and D, they'd been in the same tutorial groups at medical school. He'd seen Mathew preen when he'd had his professor's approval—and the memory of that was creating the niggle now. The way Mathew had looked at Anya when he'd introduced them…he'd seen no adoration in Mathew's eyes, just the same self-satisfaction that he'd done the right thing.

He was being kind? *Bleurgh.*

Cut it out, he told himself. Mathew's marriage

was none of his business, and why a pair of smiling eyes had set him worrying... It was dumb.

He grabbed his stick and pulled himself to his feet. Dammit, there had to be something he could do.

And then Mary appeared at the door.

'Dr Duncan, can you hold the fort?' she said briskly. 'I've had a call. One of the wedding guests seems to be ill and they want me to go over.' She grimaced. 'Bertha Mayne's always one to make mountains out of molehills, but her husband's taken her out of church. He says he doesn't want to disturb Mathew. Well, I should think not, breaking up a wedding because she has gastro? But I wouldn't put it past her, so I'll go. Are you okay on your own?' And she looked—pointedly—at his cane.

'I can manage,' he said, trying hard not to grit his teeth. The hospital currently held long-term, nursing home care patients, plus two mums with newborns and three others who, in Ben's opinion, could have been discharged yesterday. Yep, he might just possibly be able to manage.

'Excellent,' Mary said briskly. 'Good luck,' she added as if she was leaving him with an emergency ward full of accident victims—and left him to it.

The church was crowded. Every one of Mathew's relations was here. Every person who'd ever helped Reyna through those long, difficult years. Every person who'd cared. There were smiles everywhere as Anya made her way down the aisle.

Her mother was by her side, and Reyna's smile was the broadest of all. Her Anya was finally settling into this community who'd cared for her. Her Anya was becoming a doctor for this town. This was her mother's happy ending, Anya thought, focusing on keeping her feet in time with the music.

She also needed to smile.

There was Mathew in his dinner suit, beaming with a smile that sometimes she thought was a trifle too self-satisfied. She tried a smile back—she should have been smiling all the way down the aisle.

'A bit slower,' her mother whispered, and suddenly the hand on her arm became heavy. Anya glanced at her and saw a sheen of sweat on her face beneath the smile.

There was a place in the front row waiting for her mum, and they were nearly there. Mathew's dad was already standing, waiting to assist her to her place. So much kindness.

And then Mathew's mum rose as well. That wasn't in the plan, surely.

'S…sorry,' she gasped, and she pushed past her husband, edged past Anya and Reyna—and she bolted for the door.

And it was as if her departure had been a signal. Others were standing, muttering apologies, pushing along the rows to reach the aisle and then almost running.

And, beside her, Reyna's knees buckled. She sank to the floor and she started to retch.

The phone was ringing at the nurses' station, but the nurses, Mike and Janet, were having tea and scones on the lawn. They'd invited him to share, but the thought had made Ben flinch. He'd wanted this locum to be a way to ease back into medicine, and tea and scones wasn't what he'd had in mind.

Ben had trained in emergency medicine. The city hospital where he'd been based before the accident was usually frantic on a Saturday afternoon. Here…not so much. But one of the nurses should be on phone duty.

The phone was on its eighth ring before he reached it, and that made him flinch again. What if it was an emergency?

Did emergencies ever happen in Merriwood?

He lifted the receiver. 'Merriwood Hospital?'

'Ben?'

It was Mary, and she sounded panicked. More than panicked. Terrified. 'You'd better get over here. Food poisoning? Norovirus? Whatever, they're going down like flies.'

'Who?'

'Half the church,' she wailed, and as if on

cue one of the nurses—Mike—came striding through from outside. Striding? More like running.

'Sorry, mate,' he gasped as he headed for the bathroom. 'Something I ate?'

'Mum?' Anya was stooped over her mother, instinctively feeling for her pulse, looking at the grey of her face.

'S…sorry.' Reyna was fighting for control. 'Oh, love… Just help me outside. Please…don't let me stop you from getting married.'

They left the hospital unmanned—or almost. Beth, the hospital cook, had just started preparation for dinner when Ben limped into the kitchen.

'Beth, we have an emergency over at the church. Possible multiple food poisoning. Are you feeling okay?'

'Never better,' Beth said. She was middle-aged, portly and unflappable. '*Food* poisoning?'

'We don't know for sure. Mike's unwell as well, and Janet and I are heading for the church. Can you cope for a bit, answer bells? Ring me if you need me.'

'Well,' Beth said, wiping her hands on her apron. 'What a to-do. Off you go, then. I can answer bells and provide bed pans with the best of them. It'll have to be cold meat and salad for tea tonight, but no one will get food poisoning on my watch.' And then she sniffed.

'It'll be that Jeanie and her *catering*,' she said with dour satisfaction, saying the word *catering* as if it were a joke. 'Her mum said she was making sushi for the pre-wedding lunch, and I'm betting that's what it is. Lorna was proud as punch that her daughter was making something exotic, but it's cooked rice. I thought where was she going to store sushi when every fridge at the hall was packed with stuff for the reception? She'll have left it out overnight, that's what I'm betting. What's wrong with sandwiches and sausage rolls? I thought, though she'd probably have found some way to stuff that up too. She's a ding-a-ling, but Mathew feels sorry for her and this is the result.'

'Beth…'

She waved her hands in dismissal. 'I know, you're in a hurry and here I am hypothesising instead of helping. Go on, get over there and fix it. Oh, my heavens, what a disaster.'

It was indeed a disaster. He and Janet took the hospital car, and as they pulled up they saw clusters of wedding guests in the church gardens, each gathered around someone kneeling or prone. There were more guests further out, where garden turned into bushland.

Beth's words were echoing in Ben's head. Sushi. Cooked rice.

She could well be right.

Bacillus cereus was one of the most common causes of food poisoning. Ben had seen it often in his work in the Emergency Department at Sydney Central. The nickname for it among the staff there was Fried Rice Syndrome. Cooked rice was one of its favourite breeding grounds.

Janet was out of the car almost before it stopped. 'Oh, my… That's my dad over there,' she threw at him. 'I'll just make sure he's okay before I…' She didn't finish the sentence before she started running.

Ben took a little more time. Initial appraisal—triage, as comprehensive as time allowed—had been drilled into him since first year medical school. *Unless someone's actively dying, don't jump in before you have a clear picture of the whole situation.* Often attention could be caught by the person screaming the loudest, when the quiet ones were the persons in most need.

So his gaze moved from group to group. At a guess, he thought, maybe one in three or four was actively ill, and they were generally being supported by those who weren't. Maybe they hadn't been at the lunch or hadn't eaten sushi.

What he needed right now was a megaphone. He didn't have one. Okay, channel your inner football coach.

'People, I need your attention.' He made his voice as booming as he could manage, and was reasonably satisfied as heads swivelled.

'I'm Dr Duncan,' he told them. 'I'm standing in for Dr Cummins.' Where was Mathew? Still getting married? And was Doc Mary inside the church? 'My first thought here is that we're dealing with food poisoning, maybe food that wasn't refrigerated properly.' He was using Beth's untested hypothesis, but it could help. People would be familiar with tummy bugs caused by off food, and an explanation could ease panic.

'So it's unpleasant but it'll pass,' he continued, still in his booming voice. 'And those who didn't eat whatever it was can't catch it. What I want you all to do is look out for each and every one of our sufferers. The most important thing is to make sure no one's breathing is blocked—every one of you, that's your biggest job. Also reassure everyone that it's just something they ate, and it'll pass. Janet'll be moving around outside. I'll check those inside the church and then come out to help. I assume Dr Carmichael's in there? I'm not sure if Dr Cummins is...'

'If it is food poisoning it'll have come from lunch,' someone called. 'And Mathew was somewhere with his mates and Anya was having her hair done.'

'Great, that means we'll have every medic able to help,' he said. 'Okay, people, take care of everyone else, and if you're worried, call for help. Loudly. One of us will be with you in moments.'

And in the church…

All around her was chaos. Guests were sitting white-faced in the pews clutching their stomachs while their companions hovered, wondering how to help. A beefy farmer was roaring at someone to get out of the bathroom leading off the vestry, hammering on the door. Mary Carmichael was trying to help eight months pregnant Louise Hoffman. Anya could hear her over the noise—'Jim, lift her up, we'll get her across to the hospital but I'm pretty sure these cramps will be from the tummy bug, not the baby coming.'

And on the carpeted floor of the aisle lay her mother.

Reyna had retched once, and then slumped. Her face had lost all colour. Anya had caught her as she'd fallen, lowered her, glanced up and seen others leave clutching their stomachs.

And then Reyna's face had changed to another colour. A deathly blue.

'Mum!' She didn't scream out loud, but she screamed inside. She was a doctor. She knew this colour.

Where was her pulse? Where?

She was hauling her mother's pretty scarf from around her neck, fighting to clear her mouth, searching for any signs of breathing. Her breathing wasn't blocked. It was just…not there.

Mum!

Her heart. CPR! Dear heaven, she needed help. She was trying to rip her mum's blouse, fighting to be a doctor, fighting not to be a terrified daughter. Please, no! Why didn't this blouse rip?

And then another figure was standing over her—and then crouching. Ben.

'There's no…she's not breathing.' It was all she could do to say it.

'You're sure?'

'Yes.'

'Then clear her airways and breathe for her,' he snapped. 'Leave the compressions to me.' He was grabbing the sides of her mum's blouse and ripping with one sharp pull. 'Breathe, Anya, do it.' His hands were already cupped and pushing down.

The rest of the world had to be blocked out. Even if this wasn't her mum, this was first priority. Cardiac arrest…

It *was* her mum.

Block it out.

Two breaths every fifteen compressions. Breathe. Count. Breathe. Count.

Mum, breathe yourself. Please…

'Mary!' Ben's voice reverberated up to the rafters of the church, cutting through the chaos as he yelled to Dr Carmichael. His hands didn't stop their rhythmic pumping. 'You have your phone? Ring the hospital and get a defibrillator over here, fast. Tell Beth to leave what she's doing and break the speed limit. Cardiac arrest!'

That caused a sudden shocked hush in the little church. Even those actively retching seemed to stop, mid retch.

'I've killed everyone. I've killed everyone!' It was an appalled scream from the middle of the church, followed by hysterical sobs. Jeanie. Mathew's friend. Wedding caterer.

But Anya wasn't focusing on Jeanie. Thirteen, fourteen, fifteen, breathe…

The sounds in the church were becoming a muted buzz. All she could hear was the counting in her head. Mum!

It was too long. Far too long with no response.

Someone—Beth?—came flying in with the defibrillator. Pads.

Attach. Shock. Repeat.

Nothing. Nothing worked.

She'd lost her mum.

CHAPTER TWO

THE REST OF the day passed in a blur of medical necessity. And grief.

And Mathew was nowhere.

Not that Anya noticed. She was beyond noticing anything but what was in front of her.

In those first few minutes Ben cleared everything from her way. She accompanied her mother's body back to the hospital. She sat beside her for a numb half an hour or so, when her mind simply wouldn't function, and then somehow she emerged. She closed her mind to shock and horror, she pulled off the stupid wedding gown and left it in a heap in the hospital laundry, she donned theatre scrubs and somehow she pulled her mind back into medical mode.

Both Mary and Ben were working at full pace—or faster. So was Janet. The nurse glanced at Anya's face, flinched, gave her a swift, hard hug and then asked the question.

'Sweetheart, can you work? This is beyond awful, but Ben and Mary are up against it. It's definitely gastro, though. Everyone ill seems to have eaten the sushi.'

Anya took a deep breath and somehow fought back all thoughts of her mother. That had to wait. For now, she had to be what she was. A doctor.

'What needs doing?'

'The younger ones have mostly headed to their own bathrooms,' Janet told her. 'But Ben's said no one's to go home alone. If there's no one to care for them then they stay here. He's co-opted people to do one-on-one care, yelling if they need us. Ben's worried about...' She faltered and then continued.

'Well, he's worried about someone else collapsing like your mum. We've set up a supervision area on the veranda and Mary's setting up drips. But it's Louise Hoffman who's the most concern. The cramps seem to have pushed her into full labour and she's ill as well. There's signs the baby's stressed...the heart rate's dropping. Ben wants to do an emergency Caesarean, but Mary's also nauseous. Apparently Jeanie dropped sushi off at the staffroom and Mary had a taste for lunch. Not much, she says, and she's only queasy, but giving an anaesthetic to someone liable to retch is... Well, Mary says she needs total focus and if she's nauseous she doesn't trust herself to do it. We wondered...can you...could you possibly act as anaesthetist?'

'Where's Mathew?' Anya stared at Janet in bewilderment.

'We think he took Jeanie home,' Janet said in a voice carefully devoid of judgement. 'Someone said…she's not ill but she's upset. Mathew's not answering his phone.'

The two women stared at each other. Said nothing.

'I see,' Anya said at last. She closed her eyes for one brief moment. She regrouped.

And then she went to help Ben deliver a baby.

Half an hour ago Ben had left her at her mother's side, in full bridal wear, crumpled and sobbing, gutted to the core by the shock of her mother's fatal infarct. Now she entered Theatre and she was already dressed in scrubs.

Her face was swollen from weeping, but it was washed, devoid of bridal make-up. A simple band held her soft, dark curls away from her face. Her face was drained of colour. She looked almost haggard, but her expression was set.

'Louise.' She went straight to the table and took the young mum's hands in hers, ignoring everything around her in the face of Louise's distress. 'I'm here to help, as backup to Dr Duncan. I'm so sorry you've copped this. A tummy upset and a baby all in the one day—wow!' And then, somehow, she managed to recreate that smile he'd seen when he'd first met her, the smile that was as reassuring as it was warm.

'The good thing is though, Louise, that by the time your tummy settles you'll have your gorgeous baby to cuddle while you recover. It's a little girl, isn't it? How lovely. And Jim…' She turned to the big man sitting, white-faced and silent, in a corner of Theatre. 'No tummy bug problems for you?'

'I never eat sushi,' Louise's husband said in a voice that was tight with strain. 'Louise ate heaps.'

'Don't talk about sushi,' Louise moaned.

'No, let's talk about babies,' Ben said, glancing again at Anya and thinking this woman must have courage in spades. The transformation from grief-stricken bride to efficient and reassuring doctor was astonishing. 'Anya, I assume you're here to give the anaesthetic?'

'If I can't get married today, next best thing is delivering a baby,' she said, and there was that smile again. Dear heaven, the courage of the woman.

Neither Louise nor Jim could have heard about Anya's mother, Ben thought, and Anya would realise that this needed to be a birth scene, where death had no place. Cheer, therefore, had to be summoned, and confidence, and Ben watched in awe as Anya almost visibly pulled those two together.

'Janet's told me why the Caesarean,' Anya was saying. She cast a glance at Ben as she talked, and he saw in that glance that she knew the urgency. The baby's heart rate was dropping to a dangerous level and Janet must have briefed her before she'd entered Theatre. 'I assume you're already scrubbed?'

'I have.'

Janet was moving into gear, setting up the screen so Louise—and Jim—would have no vision of the preparation for incision. An incubation crib was ready at the side. He had everything at hand. He'd already briefed Janet on how to handle the newborn if it was distressed.

'Right, give me three minutes to wash up and we're ready to go,' Anya told him, still with her eyes on his. All sorts of medical questions were being asked and answered in that look. Like how bad was it? Like was there anything else she needed to know?

'We've given metoclopramide a few minutes ago,' Ben told her, meeting her look full-on. 'That should stop the retching. We're under control as long as you're happy giving a general. We'll be ready—if you are?' And that was a question he had to ask.

'I'm ready,' Anya told him, their gazes still locked, and then she looked back at Louise. 'Is it okay if I pop you to sleep for just a few minutes? I know you'd like to stay awake, and I get that, but it's such a bad look—your little one wants to greet a warm, smiley mum, not one with her head in a bucket.'

And Louise gave her a shaky smile. 'Please, keep my head out of the bucket,' she whispered. 'Just give me my baby.'

He was good. He was very good.

Performing an urgent Caesarean on a mum who was compromised with gastro was a hard call. What Anya would have preferred—what she desperately wanted—was a full theatre of trained staff. A gynaecologist with surgical skills, with more surgical backup behind. A neonatal paediatrician to receive the baby. A fully trained anaesthetist who could cope with a mother who was liable to vomit at any moment.

Her training had included this, but Caesars were rarely performed in Merriwood—a bigger hospital with a full complement of specialists was only an hour away. So her skills were rusty, but she had no choice.

Given her druthers, light sedation and a spinal block might have been the preferred option, but for a vomiting patient it could have resulted in a messy disaster. What was needed was a general anaesthetic—but a light one—with the insertion of an endotracheal tube to prevent aspiration of any vomit. This level of anaesthesia was normally outside Anya's professional comfort zone, but with Ben she felt fully in control.

Ben was in control.

She knew his background was emergency medicine, not obstetrics, but there was no hesitation in his work, no hint that he didn't perform Caesars every day of his working life.

Many obstetric surgeons asked dads to stay outside during a general anaesthetic, but Jim was given the option to remain. Outside there was no staff member to offer a cup of tea, to make sure panic didn't set in, and Jim had already coped with vomit, with mess. When Ben offered him the option to wait outside he knocked them back with grim determination. 'I'm staying with my girls!'

So he stayed, white-faced and silent, while Ben worked swiftly, expertly, surely.

And he was an expert. His fingers were fast and sure, and he worked with total confidence that all would be well. And as he worked he kept up a running commentary for Jim. Steady, professional words that resounded around the theatre, that promised all would be well.

And finally...

'Two minutes and she'll be all yours,' Ben said at last and then, 'Hey, little girl, welcome to the world.'

And instead of panic there was a happiness. A happiness that flooded the theatre, as one healthy little girl was raised from her mum and even managed a glorious, healthy mew of protest.

Anya didn't have time to weep, but if she had the tears would have been from mixed emotions.

Something good had come of this night. No, something great. A new little life.

The anaesthetic was reversed. The intubation tube was removed. The thing was done.

'Th…thank you,' Louise quavered as she surfaced, as a now beaming Jim proudly placed their daughter into her arms, as their world settled.

But Ben shook his head. 'No thanks required,' he told them. 'This has been an absolute joy.'

And Anya could only agree.

The night settled. The drama was over, for the whole town. The gastro attacks had been sharp and short. Whatever it was that had caused the reaction seemed to have faded by nightfall.

Louise's baby was perfect, her heart rate settling almost the moment she was born. Baby Elizabeth was currently asleep in Jim's arms, and Louise was asleep as well. Jim wasn't sleeping—he wasn't even thinking of being tired. He was sitting in an armchair at his wife's bedside, holding his daughter and gazing at his little family with awed bliss. Tomorrow the drama of gastro would simply be part of the birth story.

And Anya returned to say goodbye to her mother.

Reyna's body hadn't been shifted to the morgue. Someone—it must have been Ben, because somehow he'd become doctor in charge—had decreed that she shouldn't be moved until Anya had had all the time she needed to sit with her. Finally Anya was able to weep as she needed to, and to let the events of the day replay in her head.

The awfulness of losing her mum. That was the worst, and it needed to be faced, but it was too big a grief to take in completely. Instead, as she sat by her mum, as she felt Reyna's presence slowly slip away, what had happened during the rest of the day settled in her confused mind.

Her mum's joy as she'd helped her dress. That was a memory that would last for ever.

Then the church. Seeing Mathew at the end of the aisle. Strangely also she remembered... the doubts.

But then she remembered the feel of her mum's hand in hers, the quiet pressure to walk forward. Her mum's happiness.

The expectant faces of the wedding guests.

And then the chaos.

Ben, taking charge. The awful emptiness as realisation of her mum's death had sunk in.

But then glimmers of something else. A tiny baby. The look of joy on the new parents' faces. The way they'd looked at each other.

Their love.

Ben's gentleness. Janet's hug as they'd stood back and watched the new little family come together.

So many emotions. Everything was out of kilter. It was like a kaleidoscope, image after image superimposed on each other.

Trying to distract herself, she picked up the chart someone had put on the bedside table—as if it could still matter. Reyna's medical history.

She leafed through it—and then she froze.

No.

It was too much to take in. She would not—*could not*—think about it.

She focused again on her mum. She held that cooling hand and let herself weep as much as her body demanded.

Finally she rose to leave, but before she left she had one final thing to tell her mother.

'I can't marry Mathew, Mum,' she said, softly but surely. 'I'm sorry, but I'm over being grateful. I know he was kind to us, the whole town was kind to us—but you and I have more than repaid our debt. I'm glad you saw me being the bride you wanted me to be, but from now on... Mum, I'm on my own and I don't want to be indebted ever again. Thank you, Mum, for giving me so much. I'll love you for ever.'

Then she bent and kissed her mother's face. She blinked back the tears she was determined to no longer shed until she was safely home, and then she walked from the room and closed the door.

What next? She was having trouble focusing but she needed to make sure things were done for the night, that Mary and Ben were safely in charge.

Ben. His presence today had been a godsend. She'd been incredulous when Mathew had hired him—'Why do we need a locum when Mary's more than willing to take over?' but right now she was overwhelmingly glad he had.

Where was he? She turned and headed for the nurses' station, and there he was.

'Anya.' He turned from the front desk, looking calmly professional, setting down a chart he'd been reading. 'All's well in the wards,' he told her. 'Mary's gone home to bed but she's okay. I'm on call during the night and Mary's capable of backup if needed, but everything's quiet.'

'Where's…where's Mathew?' She didn't actually want to know, but she had to ask.

'He's still not answering his phone. It doesn't matter. We have things covered.' He hesitated. 'Can I drive you home?'

And then her phone pinged with an incoming text. She lifted it and saw Mathew's name.

For a moment her gut instinct was to toss the phone into the wall. The events of the day had been overwhelming, the chart she'd just read had left her feeling sick to her stomach, and her reaction now was an almost visceral revulsion.

Ben was watching her. Smashing her phone would achieve nothing. She forced herself to read.

With Jeanie. She's so upset I'm having to medicate her. But I've just heard about your mum. I'm so sorry. I'll be with you as soon as I can.

She stared blindly at the screen—and then she stared up at Ben. He gazed back, looking concerned. Was he reading another disaster in her expression?

No. This wasn't a disaster. This was just the end of a very long day.

The end of…a lot.

'I need to make a call,' she told him.

'I'll leave you to it.'

'No.' On impulse she stopped his instinctive retreat. 'Ben, please…if you will… I know this sounds dumb, but for some reason…will you listen? I think… I just need someone to be here while I do this.'

'Sure,' he said, sounding confused but still concerned.

It was dumb to hold him here. She knew that, but her knees seemed like jelly and maybe…

maybe Ben's presence might help her say the words that needed to be said.

Mathew answered on the second ring. She'd turned the phone to speaker, so his voice rang out in the corridor as if he were here in person. 'Love…'

She cut him off. The last thing she needed right now was sympathy.

'Mathew, why didn't you tell me Mum's heart problem was worsening?'

That was followed by silence—and Anya let it hang. The silence helped her as well, settling what she needed to do. In her mind was the information on the chart in Reyna's room, the chart she'd picked up almost automatically.

She'd been three things today, a bride, a grieving daughter and a doctor, and of all of those things, medicine was what gave her time out. So she'd read the chart.

And now she stood and waited for Mathew's answer. Which was taking a long time coming.

'Her history's there,' she said. 'Ben must have asked for it, or maybe one of the nurses grabbed it. I don't know. But I just read it. You sent her to a specialist three weeks ago—it must have been while I was at the conference in Sydney. Did your mum take her? I guess she did, your mum's always kind. But the report's there. Recommendation, immediate cardiac bypass surgery. And the report came to you. Did you tell her, Mathew? Did you? Because you sure as hell didn't tell me.'

And she could no longer hold it back. Anger, deep within, was coiled so tight it felt like a hard, tangible ball.

'Of course I told her. But we thought…'

'Who thought?' She was vaguely aware of— and somehow held steady by—Ben's presence. He was still with her, leaning against the wall, his hands in his pockets, calmly watching.

Strangely, it helped, to have this dispassionate bystander as mute witness. Or as quiet support? That was what it felt like, and it was the one crumb of comfort in this whole mess. That Ben hadn't turned his back on her.

Was he, too, being kind? No, she decided. He was being professional. Grieving daughter in the hospital corridor, ready to explode with anger. Professionally, he was probably mentally loading a syringe with tranquilliser. Wondering which hospital bed he could put her in tonight.

'We thought it was best,' Mathew said at last, sounding miserable. But then he seemed to regroup, and his voice took on a trace of belligerence. 'She and I discussed it, but it didn't seem so urgent that she needed surgery straight away. I told her it could probably wait until after the wedding.'

'*Probably?*'

'It was a joint decision. Your mum agreed it

wouldn't have been kind to worry you when we were about to leave on our honeymoon.'

'And so she died.' Her voice sounded weird.

'Love, I know it's awful, but long-term…you know your mum had end stage renal failure. Everything was starting to shut down. Your mum was so happy to see you married, so maybe… maybe this quick death was a blessing. I know you can't see it now—you must be devastated. I feel your pain.'

'You don't feel my pain,' she whispered, and for some reason she glanced at Ben. Amazingly, Ben nodded, as if he approved. How could he? But that nod…somehow it helped her find the strength to say what had to be said.

'Mathew, I don't want to marry you.'

Another silence. He'd be incredulous, Anya thought, in the small space in her head that was capable of considering what he'd be feeling. Mathew was the town's biggest prize, the golden boy, the guy who'd taken an impoverished kid and given her so much…

'Why not?' he said at last.

And somehow she had to suppress her fury, to make herself say the words that had been forming in her heart…for how long? Maybe for ever.

'Because you're kind,' she managed at last. 'You've been kind to me for most of my life, but Mathew, from now on you can take me off your list of charitable causes. I'm not marrying you. It's over.'

And before he could say another word she disconnected. Then she stood, staring at the floor, trying to figure what came next. She needed to go home, she thought. Home—without her mum?

Finally, she looked up at Ben again and found him still calmly watching.

'I'm sorry,' he said gently but she shook her head.

'Don't be. Telling him that has been the one good outcome of a horrible day. I should have done it years ago but…but it would have hurt too many people.'

'I can see that,' he said, and she met his gaze and thought that somehow he did.

'Can I drive you home?' he asked, and she made her fuzzy mind consider. It was a kindness that he'd offered, and right now she wanted kindness like a hole in the head, but she could accept this.

'Mum… Mum and I arrived here in the wedding limo,' she told him. 'My car's at home, so yes, please, I'd like you to drive me home. I'm… I'm done here.'

CHAPTER THREE

BEN DROVE ANYA home in silence. Apart from terse directions, she said nothing, just stared rigidly ahead. When they reached the house, he pulled up and watched her stare out of the car window and almost visibly brace.

The moon was full and the front yard was almost as well-lit as in daylight. He could see stuff sitting on her front porch. Bunches of flowers. What else?

'They'll be casseroles,' she said dully, staring out at them. 'Multiple tuna bakes. Already.'

'In the middle of such chaos?'

He couldn't believe it. A wedding abandoned, half the town with food poisoning, and there were still those who'd thought of Anya and dashed home and cooked a casserole.

'People are...' She hesitated.

'Kind. I get it. But so fast?'

'Kindness is an involuntary reflex in this town. It's always been that way. I'm...'

'Grateful?' He looked out at the pile of casseroles and then looked back at her face. The closed look. The pain.

'You want me to cart them away and ditch them in the river?'

There was a moment's silence and then she swivelled in the car to stare at him—as if she were looking at a patient who'd taken a few too many drugs and she was assessing where on the scale of crazy he was sitting. And then her face cracked a little and she choked out something very like laughter. Which sort of ended in tears.

But the tears weren't permitted to flow. She swiped her hand across her eyes and when she spoke she seemed to have herself under control. Sort of.

'Thank you, but no,' she told him, and she almost managed to suppress the wobble in her voice. 'I'll need to give all the containers back, carefully washed, with thank you notes attached. The locals would be offended if they saw their beloved Tupperware containers floating downstream.'

'It might, though,' he suggested thoughtfully, 'give you some satisfaction, setting them free.'

'I couldn't be so...' he heard the strain as she almost forced herself to say the word '...ungrateful.'

There was a moment's silence while he thought about saying something. But then he gave an inward shrug. The strain on her face... He could hardly make things worse.

'Janet told me a little about your background,' he said softly. 'She told me how good Mathew's been to you. She added a few more facts while we were assessing baby Elizabeth. Janet thinks Mathew's been oppressively good.'

'Does Janet think that?' She shook her head, looking dazed. She hardly saw him, he thought. 'I guess,' she whispered. 'Janet's an outsider as well,' she whispered. 'She's a single mum of teenage boys. She came home ten years ago to nurse her ageing parents. Maybe she's been the recipient of Mathew's kindness too.'

'Haven't we all?' Ben said grimly. 'You don't really think Mathew needed a locum.' It was okay to talk about this, he thought. Anything to give her a break from the overwhelming grief. 'Did he tell you I was in a car crash twelve months back? I've been out of medicine since, while I've struggled with my wife's death and rehab from spinal injuries. Mathew thought this would be a kind way to break me back into medicine.'

'He didn't tell me,' she whispered. 'But... I'm so sorry.'

'Don't you dare be sorry,' he said, suddenly harsh. 'I'm over *sorry*, like you're over *grateful*.'

'I...yes. I guess.' There was another silence. She stared at him and then closed her eyes for a millisecond, before turning again to the car door. Ready to go into that silent house alone.

And he couldn't bear it.

He looked again out at the pile of casseroles and winced. She didn't want him to be kind, he thought. He got that—he knew too well how unbearable continual charity could seem. So he understood, but he was also remembering a silent house, an aching void, and he knew he had to do something.

'So what say we head to the river and feed all these casseroles to the fish?' he said.

The car door stilled, half open. 'We can't.' She sounded bewildered.

'Yes, we can.' Then, as she turned to stare at him again, he tried a smile. What he wanted was to make things okay for her, but there was no way he would—or could. Her grief was her own, not to be intruded on. But this way…

'Maybe tossing casseroles would be cathartic for both of us,' he suggested, thinking of logistics. 'It's a full moon so we should be able to see, and with the chaos in this town there'll be no one around. I have a prescription pad in my bag. We can feed the fish, then pop a script, with descriptions, into each container, so you can write thank-you notes at your leisure. If I'd thought, I'd have pre-purchased some flowery notepaper so we could have done thank-you letters on the spot, but we'll just have to make do.'

There was a moment's stunned silence while she thought about it. While he stayed silent, hoping that appalling look of grief might ease just a little.

'You're crazy,' she said at last.

'Maybe we both are a little,' he agreed. 'Mine's a backburner of crazy. Yours…a catastrophe of a wedding and your mum's death. Anya, if you can't be crazy tonight, then when can you be?'

'Thank you, but I…can't,' she said and then she turned and stared back out at the casseroles. 'There must be a dozen or more casseroles out there.'

Ha! He had her. This was a moment's thought of something besides confusion and grief. 'Will there be any good ones?' he asked.

And the moment expanded. 'The tuna bakes, not so much,' she admitted. 'There's a generic recipe everyone seems to use, and who really likes pineapple with tuna? But I'm betting Mrs Hornby will have produced her lasagne. That's been voted by the town as the best this side of Italy.'

'Then if you don't want it, I'll take it,' he said promptly. 'Or we'll share. I'm living in hospital accommodation, with only a microwave for company.'

Amazingly, that was enough to produce a gurgle of choked laughter. It sounded…good. It sounded free.

'Should I add that in my thank you note to Mrs Hornby?' she managed. 'That Dr Duncan was grateful as well as me?'

'No,' he said, suddenly very, very serious. 'Dr Duncan is done being grateful, and by the sound of it so are you. Now, let's get things moving. We have a river full of hungry fish, just waiting for a tuna bake.' And then he paused as a discordant thought hit him. 'Hang on. Tuna bakes… Fish… We're not encouraging them to be cannibals, are we? Or doing something environmentally appalling?'

She shook her head, suddenly determined. 'How can we be? Big fish have been eating little fish from time immemorial. Besides, most of the fish upstream are carp, and they're taking over from native fish. There's a station downstream to catch and remove them. It'll make them slower and fatter, easier for the Fisheries people to catch.'

'How excellent!' Then, as he saw the strain behind the attempt to smile, because he didn't seem to be able to help himself, he reached out and touched her cheek. It was a feather touch, the merest trace of human contact, but he wondered as he touched her why he seemed to need it as much as he sensed she did.

'There you go,' he said in a voice that was suddenly a bit unsteady. 'The casseroles won't have been baked in vain. Let's go do a community service. Do you think anyone will be grateful?'

'They'd better not be,' Anya managed. 'Because like you said, I'm done.'

'Yep, grateful is so last week,' he agreed. 'Let's move right on.'

It was the weirdest night.

Her wedding was off.

Her mother was dead.

By rights, she should be curled up in bed, huddled in a cocoon of shock and grief. Instead, she was standing knee-deep in the pebbly shallows in the midst of the Merriwood river.

Ben was on the bank. He'd produced a lantern from the boot of his gorgeous vintage Morgan. 'You drive a car like mine, you need to be prepared for running repairs in the dark,' he'd told her. He was now carefully inspecting casseroles, writing details in his pad and then bringing them out to where she stood in the shallows.

Her job was to scrape them out, making sure they didn't drop into the water in a lump, but scattering their contents, so the fish could easily feed and there was no way a Merriwood local could come upon a hearty wedge of tuna bake washed up on the bank the next morning.

The water she stood in was cold—icy in fact. She'd grabbed a jogging suit before she'd left home. Her sweatshirt was warm but her rolled-up pants left her feet freezing.

She hardly noticed. She and Ben weren't talking. They were simply acting automatically.

It was almost like operating, she thought, like standing in Theatre. If she was the surgeon, Ben would be the assistant, providing what she needed without having to be asked.

And maybe he *was* providing what she needed. He'd offered to be the one out in the water, but his offer had been tentative. Maybe he'd guessed that standing knee-deep in the shallows, listening to the water ripple gently over the stones, letting the moonlight glimmer through the eucalypts and play on her face…after the chaos of the day, this was balm.

No, not balm, she thought as she let the latest casserole disintegrate in her fingers. Her mother's death was still there, real and dreadful. Reality would slam back soon enough. This was simply time out, a breathing space she desperately needed.

Ben was wading out to her now, his pants rolled up as well. He was limping but he'd left his cane on the bank. She could see a band of scarring on his left arm as well as on his leg— how badly had he been hurt in that car accident? Should he even be here? His feet must be as cold as hers, but he didn't seem to notice. He took the empty container from her and replaced it with a full one.

'Yep, it's another tuna bake,' he said morosely. 'I'm thinking we have about an eighty percent hit rate.'

'I read a murder mystery once,' she managed, and was astonished to hear a touch of lightness in her voice. 'A widow was finally nailed for murder when her freezer broke down and defrosted. For ten years her husband's body had lain undiscovered, covered with layer upon layer of tuna bakes.'

He chuckled, a rumbly, deep chuckle that added to the strange sensations of the night. And with it…a sliver of something unrecognisable pierced through her grief and shock. For some dumb reason Ben seemed to be enjoying himself, and that enjoyment let her feel lighter.

How could this man's smile make her feel… make her feel…?

That she had no idea how she was feeling.

But she had little time for introspection. He was examining the empty container, swishing it under the water again to make sure there were no remains. Finally, he waded out and went to fetch the next. Then the next.

Finally, he called out, 'That's it. All done until tomorrow's batch. Now, what are you planning on doing with the flowers?'

The flowers. They'd been piled by the door

as well. She'd have to cope with them when she got home.

She had a sudden visceral memory of the days after her father had died. She'd been five years old and her memories were blurred, but she did remember the flowers, so many their smell was overpowering. She remembered her mother, almost shadow-like, walking from loaned vase to loaned vase, carefully topping up the water of all of them.

'People have been so generous,' she remembered her mother saying, over and over, like a mantra. 'We can't just let them die.'

Why was she thinking of that now? Regardless, she was, and her silence must have lasted too long.

'You know, when my wife died people brought flowers to our home,' Ben said into the stillness. The rippling water was a murmuring backdrop which seemed to make everything less personal. 'I was unconscious at the time—three weeks in an induced coma and even plastic flowers would have been tempted to wilt. But apparently there were flowers a mile high piled up at our front door. So finally a few of my mates decided to collect them and they had a memorial service of their own.'

'A memorial service…?'

'Well, sort of,' he told her. 'They waited for a decent surf and an outgoing tide, then headed to the cliffs off Coogee Beach. They got rid of every piece of wrapping and then set them all free. They made a video for me to see when I was well enough, and that's how I remember them—a wash of flowers flowing out to sea.'

And then, when she didn't answer—she didn't know how—he looked thoughtfully at the rippling water. 'Maybe not here,' he said. 'They'd wash back through the town—not a good look. But we could check the tide. If it's outgoing, we could release them from the headland and they'd be out to sea and gone. Only if you're interested, of course, but it's an option.'

'But…' She stared. 'All of them?'

'Why not?'

'I… Visitors.'

Her mother's words came back to her. *People have been so generous.*

'People will come,' she whispered. 'If their flowers aren't there…'

'Are you really thinking of entertaining visitors over the next few days?' he asked. 'Do you want them? You could play the jilted bride as well as the bereaved daughter. Miss Havisham has nothing on you when it comes to having the right for isolation to be respected.'

'I…' She stared at him, stunned. 'How…?'

'Easy,' he said lightly, but there was empathy behind the lightness. Warmth. An understanding of the bewilderment this day's events had caused? 'We can paint a cross on your front door—didn't they do that in the olden days? Along with a brief note—something like *Intruders Will Be Shot!*—and no one will dare darken your door. They'll therefore assume you're grieving in a home awash with floral tributes, with their bunch front and centre.'

And up it bubbled again, a choke of laughter that was surely absolutely inappropriate. How could she be laughing on such a night? But as the laughter settled she thought again of her mum, her face set and grim, carrying her watering can from vase to vase.

Why was that memory so strong?

'Let's do it,' she whispered.

He looked at her for a long, long moment, giving her time.

'Anya, I need you to be sure,' he said softly. 'Don't let me put my ideas above what you think is the right thing. I'll help you find enough jam jars to hold every flower if you want. I'm the last person to bully you into doing something you don't want. Or to guilt you. You have no need to do anything out of obligation to me.'

There it was again, that flicker of something she didn't understand. Recognition? That didn't make sense.

But he was waiting for her to decide and, whatever strange sensations she was feeling, her way was suddenly clear. 'Mum'd love it,' she said softly. 'I know I sound ungrateful. These flowers, these casseroles, they've all been given with love and I'm incredibly grateful to have such support—Mum and I have always been grateful—but when I think of this night… We could…let the flowers go as…as maybe I need to let Mum go?'

And then, as her voice thickened with tears, she forced herself to continue.

'I need to remember this night with peace,' she told him. She looked across at the riverbank, at this man, surrounded by empty casserole containers, who was smiling gently, encouragingly at her to make her own decision—no judgement here—and suddenly she found herself smiling back.

'Today was a nightmare,' she whispered. 'Right now I can feel Mum's approval in what we're doing, and maybe even…in time…maybe she'd finally understand my decision to ditch Mathew. And who knows? I might eventually even remember tonight with a touch of laughter.'

They released the flowers from the headland beyond the town. Ben stood back and watched, a silent sentinel as the flowers scattered on the moonlit surf, then drifted outward and off to the open sea. Anya watched them go, saying nothing.

She must be overwhelmed, he thought, but

there was nothing more he could do. He simply waited until the last flower was gone. Finally, she seemed to brace herself and then turned to him.

'That was…okay,' she said simply. 'I'm ready to go.'

He drove her home. He walked her to her front door, she inserted her key and then she turned back to him. 'Thank…'

'No,' he said, cutting her off, and once more he touched her face, a feather touch, a gesture of contact that he seemed to need as much as she did. 'No thank you. No gratitude. Tonight was almost as much for me as it was for you. Mathew invited me to be locum here out of sympathy, and for some reason tonight I finally felt that I've moved on.' And in a way he suddenly realised that it was true.

Releasing the casseroles, releasing the flowers—he hadn't been able to do anything like that when Rihanna had died. But tonight, strangely, it had felt as if they were doing more than fare-welling Anya's mother.

'I'll be leaving as soon as things settle down at the hospital,' he told her. 'Or sooner. Mathew can surely cope with the aftermath of this on his own.'

'I'll be leaving too,' she whispered.

'No decisions,' he told her. 'Not tonight. Give yourself time.'

'I think,' she said slowly, 'that I've had enough time. Tonight was…right.'

'It was, wasn't it?' he said, smiling down at her. 'And if you wake tomorrow hungering for tuna bake, don't blame me.'

'There'll be more tomorrow.'

'You want me to come back tomorrow night?'

And at that she seemed to straighten. 'I can cope on my own.'

'You know, I'm very sure you can.' He touched her face again. 'Goodnight, Anya. It's been a privilege to share part of this night with you.'

And his eyes met hers for a long moment. He wasn't sure what was happening, what strange sensation was passing between them. He only knew there was no need for further words.

She gave a tiny nod, then reached up and touched his face in turn.

'Ditto,' she told him and then she turned and walked into her empty house and closed the door.

He returned to the car, drove back towards the hospital and then he slowed. Almost of its own volition the car turned towards the headland. He parked, then sat and looked out over the moonlit surf.

What now?

Something new, he thought. Enough of waiting for others to help. He should never have accepted Mathew's generous offer of this superfluous locum job. He needed to do something that was

for him, where he didn't need to thank anyone
and no one had to thank him.

Yeah, right. He was a doctor. Patients inevitably thanked him.

But even that, right now, felt as if it'd set his
teeth on edge.

So what? Give up medicine? Go find a beach
bum type of job, pouring cocktails in some fancy
beach resort?

He smiled at the thought, thinking the chances
of getting such a job would be pretty remote. His
CV—fully trained doctor with solid experience
in emergency medicine—would hardly cut it as
a barman.

But what if…?

An idea was stirring. Cocktails. Surf. Sun.
There must be a job somewhere…

The locum position at Merriwood was supposed to have been for three weeks—a low-
pressure job to ease himself back into his
high-powered position as Emergency Physician
at Sydney Central. A position where he coped
with catastrophe after catastrophe. Where lives
were saved. Where people were endlessly grateful for what he did.

Why was the thought of that gratitude
strangely unsettling? Would something like…
cocktails, surf, sun…be a way to escape the dark
thoughts that still haunted him?

Was it wrong to think of escaping?

Enough. His head was all over the place, and his leg and back ached. He needed to sleep. He'd head back to the hospital, make sure all was secure, and then he'd think about what came next.

But in his thoughts was still… Anya.

He couldn't help her, though. She didn't want more help and he got that. She'd cope. She was one strong woman.

But as he finally turned from the sea, the vision of her stayed with him. Anya, standing barelegged in the river, spooning out the casseroles, her face still blotched with tears.

Anya.

'She's nothing to do with you, mate,' he said fiercely into the night, but as the ocean disappeared behind him the memory stayed.

Anya.

CHAPTER FOUR

DID ANYONE EVER remember the details of the funerals of those they'd truly loved? Anya surely wouldn't. It was all a blur. What she'd remember would be snippets—and the way she'd felt.

The day was extraordinary. The town had pulled out all the stops to give Reyna a magnificent send-off. The church was crowded. There were flowers—so many flowers. Strangely, instead of making her feel oppressed, she loved them. They made her remember farewelling her mum down by the river, the tuna bakes, the wash of flowers heading out to sea. The true funeral?

Her mum had played the piano, and in times of deep contentment or of celebration she'd played the piece she loved best, the second movement of Beethoven's fifth concerto. For the funeral the local school band and their best piano player made an awesome attempt to get it right. Anya had asked for it, and it felt good.

The rest of the details she'd left to others. They didn't matter. Nothing seemed to matter.

She'd move on, she thought. People had told her not to make fast decisions but one was clear. The thought of staying here in her mum's house, of staying working beside Mathew…she couldn't. So maybe this funeral was more than a memorial for her mum. Maybe it was a goodbye.

Meanwhile she greeted everyone and she thanked, she thanked and she thanked. She even managed to eat two of the tiny pink jelly cakes that Jeanie produced—yes, Jeanie was doing the catering, although there wasn't any sushi in sight.

'I've saved you some,' Jeanie whispered, and when, finally, she headed for her car, Jeanie pressed a box of them into her hands. Clearly labelled 'Jeanie's Jelly Cakes'.

It was almost enough to make her smile. When she reached home she carried them to her front door, then stood, holding the box in her hands, fighting back a ridiculous longing to phone Ben. 'Hey, Ben, we have jelly cakes for the carp.'

He'd left almost a week ago. The idea was ridiculous.

But then, as the thought faded, a car door slammed and she looked out towards the street. She half expected to see Mathew. He'd been at the funeral but she'd refused to have him drive her, or sit by her. He'd been desperate to explain, to atone, to do something, but her decision was final—it had to be.

And now…it wasn't Mathew. It was someone in a gorgeous green vintage Morgan.

It was Ben—and for some reason her heart seemed to miss a beat.

'Hey.' He climbed out of the car and limped towards her, but he stopped at the front gate, as if unsure of his welcome. Or suddenly realising that it was dusk and she was alone?

She stared at him, confused. He was dressed casually, in jeans and an old leather jacket. She'd been surrounded by funeral-goers in sombre formality all afternoon. He looked good in comparison.

Actually he looked great, but that was no reason why her heart should do this weird, missing-a-beat thing.

'Before you ask, I come bearing no tuna bake,' he said before she could speak. 'Nor flowers, nor even my presence if you need to be alone. If you want, you can tell me to come back next week— or maybe never if you don't like what I'm going to suggest.' And then, as she didn't respond— she didn't know how to—he forged on.

'Anya, it seems a crazy time to approach you with such an idea, but then I thought…what better time to throw you a distraction? Regardless, like it or not, I'm here to offer you a job.'

This day was getting away from her. Carefully, as if they were infinitely fragile, she set down Jeanie's jelly cakes on the front step. 'A job?' she managed blankly.

'I know it's out of left field,' he said, and still he hadn't moved through the gate. 'But I rang Janet to find out how you were, and she tells me you've tossed in your job. So here's something to think about. I'm here to throw the prospect of a position you might enjoy, with no strings, no thanks, no gratitude attached. As a doctor on the Dolphin Isles.'

'Dolphin Isles!' She knew the place, but by reputation only. No one she knew had ever gone there.

Dolphin Isles was a gorgeous coral quay on the outer edge of Queensland's Great Barrier Reef. The biggest landmass was Dolphin Island, home to an internationally renowned luxury resort. It was too far from the mainland for day-trippers and the cost of staying in the resort was reputed to be eye-watering. A luxury resort for squillionaires.

'The job's at the island resort,' Ben was saying, while she stared at him incredulously. 'Dolphin Isles Resort. Island population three hundred. There's a small marine research centre focusing on coral rehabilitation, but the population's mostly tourists. *Rich* tourists. Because the resort's so expensive and exclusive they offer a twenty-four-hour medical service, so they're asking for a partnership. Two doctors. Once you know how much it costs to stay there, you'll know they can afford it.'

'A partnership?' Did she sound as stupid as she felt? Luckily he didn't appear to notice.

'There's been a husband-and-wife team there for the past few years,' he told her. 'An older couple who saw it as an easy lifestyle but who've finally decided to retire. So the island's used to two doctors and it wants two. With rich tourists doing what rich tourists tend to do, there'll always be swimming accidents, sunburn, overdoses—you can guess the type of thing. Plus the needs of the staff at the resort and research centre. It seems the guests the resort attracts tend to demand attention for the least scratch, and as they pander to every need someone has to be on call twenty-four-seven.'

He spread his hands. 'Anya, I'm almost ready to go back to work but I still need time to get my physical fitness back. I crushed two vertebrae in the accident and it's taking time to get myself right. I need to swim, I need a decent gym and I can't take on so much work that I can't stay focused on healing. This job sounds as if it'd suit me, and I'm applying for it. But they want two doctors, and it'd be great to find someone compatible to work with—so I thought of you.'

Her brain was struggling to take this in. She remembered, suddenly and stupidly, a cartoon she'd seen somewhere years back. A kid asking his teacher, 'Please, miss, can I go home now? My brain's full.'

Right now, her brain felt as if it might burst.

'Why…why me?' she managed.

'Why not?' he said easily. 'I've talked to the current doctors, and it sounds a doddle. You want to go live on a tropical island, lie in the sun with a little medicine on the side? There will be some genuine need, but we'll be overpaid for what we do—a population of three hundred surely can't keep two doctors frantic. Anya, best of all, we won't be doing anyone any favours. They won't be doing us any, and there should be no gratitude in sight.'

'I don't want…'

'Gratitude? Who knows that better than me?'

'But…me?' The idea made her feel dizzy. The whole day had made her feel dizzy and maybe he knew, because his voice gentled.

'Hey, I know, this is a crazy time to throw this at you, but I figured you probably wouldn't sleep anyway. And for some reason I thought it might suit us both. Why not grant yourself thoughts of tropical islands and piña coladas in between your waves of grief?'

He hesitated and his voice changed. 'Look, this is only an idea,' he told her. 'I can't work at full pace yet—this leg is still damnably weak. I also need space, and I suspect you do too. So here are the details.' And there came that smile again, gentle, beguiling—understanding?

'Think about it if you can,' he told her, and he held out a bundle of literature. 'I'm heading back to Sydney now, and I won't pressure you further. If you're interested, call me. It's only an idea, Anya. No pressure.'

'I...thank...'

'And you can cut that out.' His voice was suddenly almost savage. 'I don't like the idea of a medical partnership with someone I've never met—it'd be a downside of taking this job—so the benefits of you joining me would be mutual. But I'm applying anyway, with or without you, so there's not the least need for gratitude. This is all selfish on my part and it needs to be the same for you.'

And with that he laid the package of brochures on top of the mailbox—and he turned and limped back to his car.

Why had he done that?

Ben drove slowly back to Sydney, taking the slow coast road, roof down, enjoying the breeze on this warm night, the sense of freedom this gorgeous little car was giving him.

If he went to Dolphin Island he'd have to leave it behind.

He'd leave a lot else behind too, he thought. His parents' almost overwhelming concern. His mates' sympathy and kindness. His position at Sydney Central—they'd held it open until now, but he couldn't expect them to hold it for ever. There were bright young doctors aching to take his place.

He should mind, but he didn't. Once upon a time he'd have fought to get a position in this prestigious hospital, but right now it left him cold.

As most things left him cold.

He still wasn't sure why he was applying for Dolphin Island. He'd intended to take a couple more locum jobs before returning to Sydney Central, but Dolphin Island was a permanent position.

Was that what he wanted? A long-term career with little responsibility?

A job with Anya?

That was only a possibility, he told himself, and it was a slim one. She surely wouldn't be interested. He could have rung and asked, but the idea of taking a day and doing the lovely drive to Merriwood had been appealing.

Liar. He'd wanted to see her again. See her face. See how she was coping.

He thought of the advertisement he'd read for the job he'd told her about. *Medical Partnership on Dolphin Isles.* He'd thought of Anya working to deliver little Elizabeth Hoffman, of the way she'd thrust her grief and shock aside and worked with pure professional skill. She'd seemed an awesome doctor, compassionate and clever, and Janet had reinforced his impression of her competence. Once Janet had told him that Anya intended to leave Merriwood, it had therefore seemed logical to ask her if she was interested. It was surely much better to work with someone he knew.

But it wasn't all sense. The memory of Anya in the river, in the moonlight... The thought of her grief, her anger, her skill and her strength... The memory of the look on her face as she'd watched her mother's flowers wash out to sea... They'd merged into an image he couldn't forget.

Yeah, he'd like to work with her. He'd like to get to know her better.

Because?

Because nothing, he told himself almost savagely. It wasn't much more than twelve months since Rihanna had died. The last thing he needed was more...entanglement?

Was that what this was? More entanglement?

It was no such thing. And Anya would hardly be likely to accept, he told himself as he drove on through the night. Maybe it'd be a good thing if she didn't.

Right. Except why did that prospect feel... bleak?

CHAPTER FIVE

THE THOUGHT OF a job on Dolphin Island was so unexpected, so out of left field, so...almost crazy...that a stunned Anya, almost without thinking, rang Ben the next morning and accepted. Which was why, six weeks later, she found herself sitting in the bow of a gorgeous turquoise and gold cruiser with 'Dolphin Isles Resort' emblazoned on the side, heading to the outer rim of Queensland's Great Barrier Reef.

There'd been brochures for the resort in the information pack Ben had given her. Dolphin Island was maybe ten kilometres wide at the most, with wide sandy beaches, a centre of magnificent rainforest and a resort hidden discreetly among the trees. Its gorgeously furnished bungalows had been designed to catch the views out over the coral quays surrounding the island. A vast swimming pool, designed to look like a natural lagoon, meandered through the resort.

But as they neared the jetty she thought, as enticing as the brochure had been, it still hadn't shown this breathtaking magnificence. As the ferry drew closer, Anya was looking out at miles of turquoise water and sandy cays. A kayak was drifting outward from the island, a man and a woman on board with paddles stilled, seemingly entranced. She could see why. A pod of dolphins was cruising around them, bodies glistening in the crystal-clear water.

She glanced around and Ben was watching her, and he was grinning.

'Great, huh?'

He'd been here. The island's management had flown him over for the interview, but she gathered with his credentials and with hers, the job had almost been theirs from the start. Doctors generally looked for this type of job early, wanting a couple of years of little stress before starting their career progression. Or later when they were winding down, wanting a quiet life. For two experienced, capable doctors to apply together...

'How long did you imply that we'd stay?' she breathed, and Ben's smile widened.

'There's a three-month cooling-off period. I've left my gorgeous Morgan garaged in Sydney, just in case it doesn't work out, but of course I implied for ever.'

Why did that give her a jolt? To make her think...for ever?

It was nothing, she told herself. That was always what happened in job interviews—total commitment to the proposed position. But as he smiled at her…

For ever?

Get a grip, she told herself.

The last few weeks had been an emotional roller coaster, her grief at her mother's death overlain with the practicalities of packing a house full of memories, of saying goodbye to a town that truly had been good to them, of cutting lifetime ties.

But underneath the grief and organisational needs there'd been an undercurrent of anticipation, which right now was swelling to almost epic proportions. That first phone call to Ben to accept had been made almost without thinking, but right now she didn't regret it. She was about to land on a gorgeous tropical island with a doctor-cum-partner who seemed as kind as he was good-looking. And whose smile was…

Um…no. As the thought crossed her mind, she hauled herself back to reality with a start. Ben had just lost his wife. She'd just ditched her fiancé. They both needed time out. She needed to think of him as a medical partner, nothing else.

Meanwhile there was a guy driving a turquoise and gold luggage cart towards the jetty to meet them, and her new life was about to start.

No more ties, she told herself. No more indebtedness. She realised she was grinning back at Ben, and her smile was probably a mile wide.

'How soon for the piña coladas?' she managed, and he chuckled.

'Let's go meet the locals first,' he told her. 'It's probably not the wisest look for us to get off the boat and demand the quickest path to the bar.'

'Fair enough,' she managed but they were both grinning, two conspirators who'd pulled off something magical. 'Let's put indulgence aside for the moment—but not for long.'

The guy driving the upmarket luggage buggy introduced himself as Joe. 'I'm carter of baggage, greeter of guests, sorter of problems, general dogsbody. Anything you need, I'm your first port of call.'

Wearing shorts and polo shirt in the turquoise and gold colours of the resort, with 'Dolphin Isles Resort' emblazoned on his chest, he looked to be in his sixties, but he was wrinkled enough to seem older. Anya couldn't decide if he had indigenous heritage or if he'd simply spent a lifetime in the sun. If he had Anglo Saxon skin under that deeply tanned outer layer, she hoped he'd been checked every two minutes for skin cancers.

For some dumb reason that pleased her. Hey, I must still be a doctor, she told herself, reassured to find a sliver of professionalism inserting itself into what seemed a fantasy world.

And then they pulled up outside a bungalow, set apart from the rest of the resort accommodation. It looked gorgeous—but Joe was apologising. Its location meant if they wanted a morning swim they'd have to walk a whole hundred metres.

Oh, the hardship.

'The clinic's right next door.' Joe pointed a weathered thumb at a discreet building set to the rear of the bungalow, with a sign directing guests to Dolphin Isles Medical Centre. 'Access is coded—codes are all in your info book. I can show you through if you like, or maybe you'd like to explore yourself. Martin—our resort manager,' he explained to Anya, 'is caught up with a film crew at the other end of the island. All hush-hush of course, but you'll probably recognise the actors. That's in your contracts though, you shut up about anyone you see here. If you ask for an autograph or a selfie you'll be kicked off the island in minutes. You stay out of their faces, they stay out of yours.'

Hooray, not a chance of a tuna bake in sight, Anya thought, and she caught Ben's glance and he was looking as pleased as she was.

Joe was heaving the luggage out onto the veranda. Now he opened the door with a flourish and gestured them to come in.

'Nice place, this,' he told them. 'Nice big living room. Bathroom's the same as the resort's—outside waterfall shower but there's an inside one as well if the insect life gets a bit much. Last docs said they'd have liked a study but there's heaps of space over at the clinic if you need to work. The bedroom's just through there. Martin'll be back before dinner—he said he'll meet you in the bar at six. Meanwhile the refrigerator's stocked, make yourself at home.'

But Anya wasn't listening. She was staring at the bedroom door.

One bedroom door.

'Only one bedroom?' she asked faintly, and Joe glanced at her with doubt, maybe hearing the note of caution.

'Well, yeah. Big, though, great king-sized bed. Guess it has its problems. Doc Brenda, she's one of the docs that just left, well, she and Doc Craig had a tiff a couple of years back and Brenda slept for a whole week in the clinic. Martin reckons if he'd provided them with two bedrooms they'd still be fighting, so I guess you two need to get on. Still,' he said and grinned, 'if you can't get on here, I don't know where you can. Welcome to paradise, guys. I'll leave you to it.'

And he walked out, closing the door behind him.

Silence.

Anya walked slowly across the magnificent living room, filled with gorgeous cane furnishings, mountains of bright cushions and rugs. A vast wooden fan whirred gently overhead. There were potted plants that looked as if they'd grown there for ever, and she could see glimpses of the ocean through the palms outside. It was an awesome room—but she was focused on the bedroom door.

She walked forward and opened it. It, too, was awesome. Huge. Old-fashioned style. Another whirring fan. Gorgeous thick rugs, old-style wardrobes with Oriental carvings etched into the doors. Through the door she could see an en suite bathroom, with a stand-alone clawfoot bath, his and hers washbasins—and a door to what looked like a fernery: a shower room under the stars.

But she hardly looked at these things either. She stared instead at the truly massive bed which took up three-quarters of the room.

One bed.

'Did you see this house,' she said in a voice she hardly recognised, 'when you came for the interview?'

'I saw it from the outside,' Ben told her, sounding cautious. He obviously saw the problem. 'Brenda and Craig had their family staying from England.' He looked a bit abashed. 'Martin referred to it as the doctors' quarters, and Brenda's sister and brother-in-law were staying here as well. I guess I assumed multiple bedrooms, but maybe…they must have been using camp beds in the living room.'

'You didn't actually count the bedrooms?'

'Um…maybe not.'

There was a moment's silence while she thought this through. And then thought a little deeper. 'Did you imply to this… Martin,' she asked at last, 'that we were…married?'

'I did not.' He'd come into the bedroom behind her but there was something in his tone, something in the emphatic way he spoke, that made her wheel around to face him.

'So how exactly did you describe our relationship?'

'I did imply,' he said cautiously—very cautiously indeed—maybe sensing her loaded question, 'that we were a medical partnership. That we've been working together at Merriwood.'

She stared at him for a long moment, her mind whirling. 'Did you mention,' she said carefully, 'how long we actually worked together?'

'They didn't ask for specifics.'

'They'll surely have rung Mathew. To check on our credentials.'

There was another silence. And then, 'Mathew might,' Ben admitted, 'have been persuaded to gloss over the timing. I've told him how great this job would be for you, and he does owe you.'

'You're kidding.' The silence continued while he met her eyes, unapologetic, innocence personified.

'So,' she said at last, trying to get over the idea of Mathew's arm being twisted to deceive.

Mathew, who'd probably never told a white lie in his life. 'The advertisement for the job stated a partnership, yes? Did you check that partnership meant medical only?'

'Possibly…not.' He'd rearranged his expression and she was reminded of an ancient dog she'd fallen for on a television show she'd seen as a kid—Boris used to pinch his owner's socks and then convey—with eyes alone—that he was innocence personified.

Boris had been the reason why she'd wanted a dog.

She'd got a kitten instead.

What had she got…*instead*…now?

She had a dumb desire to laugh—but this was serious!

'So… I let you do the interview, all the arranging.' Her gaze fell to his left hand. 'And you're wearing a wedding ring.'

He glanced down at his hand. Why he still wore it he didn't know. Respect for Rihanna's parents? More protection from the truth? Whatever, this was something else he had to move on from. He twisted it off now and tossed it onto the dresser. 'I…yes.'

'Did they actually ask if we were married?'

'Maybe not,' he admitted. 'But…' his tone became virtuous again '…we have different names.'

'How many female doctors do you know

who've changed their professional names after marriage?'

'Anya...'

'Did you know?' she demanded. 'Did you suspect they thought of us as a couple?'

'I...'

'Don't you dare lie.' She glowered and his expression changed. He spread his hands. Admitting all?

'I thought this job seemed great,' he told her. 'Just what we both need. Okay, maybe I suspected they assume it, but no, I didn't lie.'

'That's so noble of you.'

'It is, isn't it?' he said, and there was that look of virtue again.

For some reason she badly wanted to giggle—but giggling was Not Appropriate.

'I'm sorry,' he said, Boris-like again, and she fought to regain her indignation.

'Yeah, that's helpful,' she said acerbically. 'So get us out of this mess. You'll explain to this Martin—and whoever else is even vaguely interested—that we're not romantically, emotionally, sexually involved. Not the tiniest, least bit. And tell them how long we actually worked together.'

He raked his fingers through his hair. It was a very ordinary gesture but it didn't seem so ordinary. It made him look...vulnerable. That and the cane he still carried.

Vulnerable? She narrowed her eyes and looked

at his penitent expression and she hardened her heart. Manipulative, more like. And, sure enough, here it came.

'Why?' he asked.

'What, why tell the truth?'

'Anya, I didn't lie,' he told her. 'If they didn't want to do their homework that's up to them. I told them I'd only been at Merriwood for a short time as a stage in my recovery, but they should check my reputation at Sydney Central. In fact, they mostly talked to Mary about your time in Merriwood.'

'Mary.' She thought about it. 'Not Mathew.'

'In the end Mary and Janet and I thought Mathew wasn't the best placed to give an over-view. I checked that he'd confirm things but that was all.'

'You talked to Mary and Janet...'

'They really wanted you to take this job.'

'You're kidding.' She glowered. 'So my friends have landed me with this?' She motioned to the ridiculously vast bed. 'Now what? You want to build a fence down the middle?'

'No need. I promise I'll keep to my side. We can share.'

'In your dreams.'

'Well...' He considered. 'I can sleep in the clinic.'

'You heard Joe. What sort of impression does that give? A warring couple? No, thanks. You can tell this Martin, whoever he is, the truth and arrange separate accommodation.'

'I doubt if there is any,' he said, his expression still hangdog. 'He told me there was a shortage of staff accommodation—too many staff and not enough rooms. And after I saw this place… Anya, I really wanted this job and I thought you would too.'

She glared at him. Then, because a glare wasn't big enough, she put her hands on her hips and assumed a megawatt glower.

'Sorry,' he said.

But there was something about that sorry. That glint behind it. A trace of laughter?

She opened her mouth to tell him where he could shove this job, this island, this whole set-up—but that twinkle gave her pause. It was almost a challenge.

She was standing in a dream house, a dream island. She had the dream job in front of her. Was she planning to walk away because this man was devious? Where would she go? Certainly not back to Merriwood.

Somewhere else as good as this?

She glowered a bit more, but her brain was suddenly suggesting practicalities. And she was also casting a surreptitious glance out of the window at the gorgeous sparkling ocean she could see through the palms. She was thinking of the kayak she'd seen. Of the dolphins.

Practicalities, she told herself. Her indignation was still full-on, but remnants of sense were intruding. Also, this view was fantastic. So…

She looked carefully around the bedroom, at the lavish but tasteful furnishings. This bed was huge—how on earth had they ever got it through the door?

On impulse she stalked forward and tugged one side of the bed. Pleasingly, it did what she'd noticed was the norm in many of the hotels she'd stayed in as a solitary medical delegate at professional conferences. The bed was on wheels but it didn't move smoothly as a single unit. She hauled off the bedlinen—and found two normal-sized double beds.

'Ha!'

'So…' Ben said cautiously, watching from the sidelines. 'Um… You're thinking we can move a bed into the living room?'

'No.' She directed another glower at him—and his dratted twinkle. 'I'm not intending to live in the bedroom while you reign supreme in the living room—and neither do I intend sleeping in the living room, with you traipsing through every time you need to go in and out. Help me separate this—and then help me move the wardrobes.'

'Wardrobes?'

'In case you hadn't noticed, we have two huge wardrobes,' she said with exaggerated patience. 'We shift them both into the middle to make a divider. One will be facing my side of the room—that'll be the side with the big window facing the ocean and with the door to the en suite—because you owe me, Ben Duncan. The other side will be yours, the side with the sliver of window up the top. You can use that dinky little bathroom off the living room. We'll have to come to some agreement over the settings of the central ceiling fan—I'm prepared to negotiate on that, but nothing else.'

'You're very...' he paused, considering '...bossy?'

'Too right, I'm bossy,' she told him and for the first time she allowed herself to smile. 'What other arrangement can work? If I meekly let you give me the best side I'd need to be grateful, and gratitude is *not* in my contract. This way you don't get to sleep in the clinic, but I'll overlook your need to be grateful. Okay, Dr Duncan, let's get on with this.'

'And Martin?' he asked cautiously. 'What do we tell him?'

'Nothing,' she said. 'I'll concede that. He doesn't get to see our bedroom. He didn't ask particulars about our relationship and it's none of his business.'

'I think housekeeping is included in our contract,' he said, still cautious.

'Then it gets taken out. You clean one week, I clean the next. We like our privacy. Right?'

'Right.' He looked at her, fascinated. 'Does that mean problems are solved?'

'For the moment,' she told him. 'Any more questions? If not, I intend to go find a piña colada. We can cope with furniture-moving later.'

And she grinned and tossed her bag on the bed—*her* bed. 'Join me if you want, but I'm heading for a drink.'

She headed for the bar. He stayed behind and did some furniture reorganisation. It was the least he could do, he decided, but also he needed a bit of space.

At the interview he'd suspected the island authorities had assumed—maybe wanted to assume—that there was a romantic link between the two of them, but he'd never been asked outright. He'd thought if it caused problems it'd be a matter of simply saying, whoops, no, professional only, to Martin and whoever else needed to be told. They could hardly sack them for not being married.

So the whoops was in reserve if anyone asked—but what was there in the sensible fallback that gave him pause?

Was it that, watching Anya's eyes flash fire, watching her incredulity and then the tiny glimmer of laughter edging in at the sides, had made him think that sharing a bedroom with her would be okay by him?

It was her laughter that had caught him. It was six weeks since her mother's death, six weeks since the catastrophe of her wedding, and yet she'd looked at this set-up, she'd listened to his pathetic excuses—yeah, he hadn't really thought this through—and he'd just known there'd been the niggle of an urge to giggle.

The woman had spirit.

He was thinking again of the night at the river, of Anya standing up to her knees in the water, of the beauty of the night, of the beauty of... Anya.

He'd wedged a mat under one of the wardrobes and was now sliding it into position. It was a decent-sized wardrobe. Two of them would make a good-sized barrier—there'd be no way they could see each other.

But there'd be no door. They could hear each other, and if...

Um...no. No, no, no. She was six weeks bereaved, plus six weeks from a disastrous non wedding. He'd put her in an invidious position by letting everyone on this island think they were a couple. One stupid move from him and he knew she'd have no choice but to walk away from this job, and this job looked like being just what she needed. And what he needed.

More, it looked like being fun.

So keep it light, he told himself, assuming a schoolmasterly tone inside his head. You're here to enjoy yourself, and that means…not enjoying yourself.

He grinned. Okay, this was dumb, tugging wardrobes was dumb, but if that was what it took he'd behave.

The bar was waiting. Anya was waiting.

He tugged the second wardrobe into place and headed out to the veranda.

To find Joe striding along the path towards him—fast. One look at his face and he knew there was trouble.

Bad trouble?

'Anya?' It was a dumb thing to think, but that was where his mind went. Anya had headed over to the bar fifteen minutes ago. What could have happened to her in that short time?

Surely nothing. But Joe was grabbing the veranda post and struggling to get his breath. He'd run?

'You gotta come, Doc,' he gasped, and made a wide gesture towards the beach. 'Coupla silly buggers on the beach…jet-skis…playing chicken, would you believe? Head-on crash. Doc Anya saw it from the bar—she's already gone. Said to get you fast, plus first aid stuff, then ring the mainland for evac. One of the kids is taking the kit down to the beach, but Doc, it looks bad. We're gonna need you.'

CHAPTER SIX

ONE MINUTE SHE'D been sitting in the bar, piña colada in hand, admiring the reflected glow of the setting sun over the sea. The next Anya was standing chest-deep in the surf, directing frightened lifeguards to help a tattooed hunk of an accident victim. At the same time she was applying pressure to try and stop catastrophic bleeding from another man's knee.

Two jet-skis had crashed headlong into each other at high speed. One man had been thrown backwards into the water; the other's leg seemed to have been smashed almost into the machine itself.

She'd seen it from the bar, two idiots doing high speed loops just out from the resort. She'd watched in dismay as a couple of young lifeguards had started yelling, waving, desperate for them to stop. She'd seen one of the riders raise what was surely a beer can at his mate, signalling…one last race?

His mate had waved in reply. The yelling from

the beach had been ignored. They'd raced in tight circles, right into the shallows, surely at impossible speeds—and then they'd ridden straight at each other.

An appalling game of chicken…

And neither side had won. Neither jet-ski had swerved.

There'd been the smash of crunching metal, a scream—and then silence.

Dear God…

'Get Ben,' she'd snapped at the barman, who was staring out at the beach with surely as much horror as she was feeling.

'Ben?'

'The other doctor. My…partner. Joe knows. Go!'

She'd been running even before she'd finished speaking. Down across the beach, through a cluster of horrified onlookers, past a couple of bikini-clad beauties standing knee-deep in the water and screaming.

A couple of kids in resort-coloured lifeguard uniforms had headed out towards the guys on the smashed machines. The jet-skis were a mangled mess. One man was in the water, the other still on what was left of his jet-ski. Blood was already clouding the water.

Thankfully—if one could be thankful for such a tiny mercy—the beach sloped at such a gentle angle that even where the jet-skis had crashed, the water was still only chest-deep.

The lifeguards had headed to the guy in the water. She was pushing her way out through the shallows, figuring where she was most needed. The crimson stain spreading around the guy still on the jet-ski made her choice for her.

From his knee down was a bloody, pulpy mess. The crimson bloom in the water suggested an artery must surely be severed. The blood was pumping. He might already have bled out.

Every second counted. She was shoving her way through the small waves, hauling her shirt off as she went. Then her pants too—even from here she knew she'd need some sort of pressure pad.

He wasn't dead, at least not yet. Slumped across the bars of his machine, he looked almost lifeless, but as she reached him he managed to stir a little.

'W...won,' he said stupidly, thickly. 'Troy's... an idiot.'

'So are you,' she said grimly, but he didn't reply. He couldn't. This amount of blood loss...

He was lying sideways across the wreck of his machine, and his oozing, bloody leg was almost clear of the water. She had no choice but to tug it upward, resting his foot on her upper arm. Then she twisted her soaked pants into a pad and shoved it as hard as she could against the source of the bleeding, fighting to find the pressure point where artery neared the bone.

The spurting flow decreased. The blood was still oozing from under her fingers but the worst of the flow seemed to have ceased.

Enough to save his life? How much blood had he lost already?

But the pad was in place. She shoved downward even harder—and then took a moment to see what was happening around her.

The two lifeguards, surely only kids, were trying to support the other guy in the water, who looked to be unconscious.

'Use a surfboard!' she yelled across at them. 'Put the board under him in the water, moving him as little as possible. I don't want his back or neck moved.' But both kids looked terrified almost to immobility. Surely they'd done this in training? They were holding the guy's head out of the water, stopping him from drowning at least, but they needed direction.

And suddenly they had it.

'Priority?' The deep call cut across the chaos, across the women's screams. And blessedly, thankfully, here was Ben, striding out through the shallows towards them. How had he got here so fast, with his bad leg? It didn't matter. He was here, he was demanding a fast update from her, his medical colleague—and she could have wept with relief.

'You go there!' she yelled. He'd be seeing the wash of crimson, which was why he was heading straight for her. 'I haven't assessed that one. But send one of the lifeguards to me.' She had to have help—she was using all her strength to keep the pad in position. One hand was under what was left of his calf, the other was pressing down, but she needed extra hands to twist tie a tourniquet.

She saw Ben pause, realising how caught up she was, and that he still needed to be in first responder mode. He cast a fast appraising glance around the scene, taking in the mess, the young kids in lifeguard gear, the huddle of shocked bystanders who'd backed off…

And then he transformed into doctor in charge. 'Apart from the lifeguards, is there anyone here with first aid training?' His voice boomed out towards the crowd of resort guests, the horrified onlookers on the shore.

A sun-wrinkled elderly woman stepped forward into the shallows. She was wearing a floral swim skirt, a matching hibiscus-covered bikini top and a gorgeous flowery swim-cap which didn't quite cover her snow-white curls.

'In between raising children I've spent thirty years as a nurse in ER,' she called, her accent markedly American. 'Retired for years, but if I can be of use…'

'Welcome back to the workforce,' Ben snapped and motioned towards Anya. 'Can you help Dr Greer? Anyone else? I need strong volunteers to get these guys to the beach. You, you and you.' He pointed as people stepped forward. 'Dr Greer's in charge at that side, I'm on the other. Take orders from either of us, we're the island medics.'

And, just like that, instead of a crowd of frightened onlookers and a couple of terrified kid lifeguards, he had a team. He was heading for the guy in the water as he spoke, and by the time people stepped forward he was already assessing.

Ben was in charge. She could focus.

The lady in the amazing swim cap had waded to her side. She was elderly, short and plump, she was up to her armpits in water, but when she spoke she sounded immediately competent.

'Dorothy Vanson,' she said briskly. 'If I can't cope with what you want me to do, I'll yell. Tell me what needs doing.'

'Ruptured artery,' Anya said, taking her at her word. 'This pad's stopping spurting but I've assessed no further. Can you check his airway?'

'Would it be better if I take over the pad?' the woman said, obviously doing her own assessment and figuring how best she could help.

'I may look old and dotty but I'm as strong as a horse. I'll push, you do the rest. You want my bikini top as a tourniquet?'

Anya blinked. 'Um…no. I think my shirt should be enough.'

'Probably for the best,' Dorothy said serenely. 'We don't want to add shock to the injuries. Okay, his foot can go on my shoulder, my hand's coming in now.'

And a millisecond later Dorothy's sun-wrinkled hand was pressing as hard as Anya had been, and Anya was free to check the guy's breathing. No obstruction there, but the breaths were fast and shallow. How much blood had he lost? Certainly enough to drop his blood pressure to dangerous levels.

What else was wrong? She couldn't assess for much else while she was in the water, but now, blessedly, she had her hands free. She could take her time to rip her shirt and make it long enough to twist into a decent tourniquet.

There were others in the water now, resort staff wading in to help, waiting for orders.

Ben was working on his guy. His makeshift team had him on a board and were carrying him towards the shore. She glanced towards the beach and saw Joe opening a massive box. A huge red cross on the side denoted it a medical kit. Equipment. Once they had these guys back on the beach their chances would increase exponentially.

But to get this guy off the jet-ski…

'I need a surfboard here too,' she called to Ben, and Ben shouted to the people on shore.

'You heard the doc, a surfboard there now, and half a dozen people to hold it steady.' And Joe himself was heading into the water, a surfboard breaking the small waves in front of him.

But his first reaction when he reached them was shock at the sight of the little lady helping. 'Mrs Vanson! You're a guest! You shouldn't be doing this.'

'So who else is going to do it?' Dorothy retorted. 'You men leave all the hard work to the women. Are you ready to shift him, Doctor?'

Anya wasn't. The last thing she wanted was to unravel him from his wreck of a jet-ski, to risk crushing a possibly injured spine, to risk opening more unexposed wounds. She couldn't stand back enough to get an overview of how he was positioned.

And then Ben was there, heading back to them but still watching the guy they were carrying towards the beach. 'Roll the whole jet-ski onto its side,' he ordered. 'Let's set the board up beside him so he slips straight on. All of you, look at the position he's in now and that's the position we want him on the board. Do it!' He glanced at Anya. 'The guy on the beach needs a trachy. Can you manage here?'

'Of course we can manage,' Dorothy said indignantly. 'You go play hero somewhere else.'

And despite the adrenalin, despite the desperate emergency, Anya found herself close to a chuckle.

Half an hour after the call they had both men stabilised. Almost. They had a tracheostomy tube in place and secure. They had drips set up, and Anya's patient's blood pressure was finally starting to rise. There were multiple fractures of face, ribs and limbs, but there were no outward signs of pierced lungs. Even better, both men were stirring into consciousness—a major indicator that they weren't facing brain damage. The problem they now faced was pain management, which was fraught when both men were obviously well affected by alcohol.

But finally, blessedly, the medical evacuation chopper appeared, swooping in fast and landing on the beach. On board was an emergency physician, two paramedics and a pilot. They took charge with competence and speed, intent on transferring the patients to the facilities of a major mainland hospital. Thus, twenty minutes after it had landed, Anya and Ben were left standing side by side, staring up at the disappearing chopper and trying to come to terms with what had just happened.

The beach had been cleared of onlookers. The resort staff were clearing the mess. Joe was escorting Dorothy and her husband back to their bungalow, apologising as he went. Obviously the Vansons were Very Important Guests and Joe was clearly horrified at their involvement.

'Oh, for heaven's sake,' Anya heard her say. 'I can't spend all my holiday lying in the sun. Henry knows I like to be busy.'

'Holiday?' Anya said faintly as they disappeared. She was still soaking wet, she was disgustingly bloodstained and she was wearing knickers plus an oversized Hawaiian shirt one of the tourists had kindly offered as soon as she'd had a chance to be aware of what she was—or wasn't—wearing. And then she added for good measure, 'Wasn't that what we were supposed to be having? A doddle? Isn't that what you offered, Dr Duncan?'

He sent her a lopsided smile. 'Whom do we sue?'

'You for a start.' She looked down at her disgusting self. 'I hope our luxury villa has plenty of hot water.'

'I hope so too.' And then his smile faded. 'Anya, you did great.'

She paused and looked at him, met his gaze and tried to figure what to say. Something flippant, she thought. Keep it light. Instead, she heard her voice wobble as the words came out.

'So did you. I can't believe you did a trachy on the beach. Awesome, Dr Duncan.'

'He looks like he has spinal damage. It'll be a long road back.'

'Yeah, and the other guy's likely to lose that leg. They won't be playing chicken again any time soon.'

'They were drunk.' Ben's voice became grim. 'And these were resort jet-skis they were using.'

'The brochure says alcohol's all-inclusive in the hotel rate.' She stared out to the shore where the remains of the wrecked jet-skis were being hauled onto a trailer. 'Those lifeguards didn't stand a chance keeping drunken idiots under control. I'm thinking…compulsory breath tests before use? The punters may not like it, but I can't see any choice.'

And then they were distracted. A short, dapper man in a navy business suit was hurrying across the sand towards them.

'Martin,' Ben said as the man approached. The resort manager?

'Ben!' The guy held out his hand in welcome—and then got near enough to see the state of them. The hand was smartly withdrawn.

'I wouldn't touch me either,' Ben said. 'Martin, this is Anya.'

'Pleased to meet you, Dr Greer,' Martin said,

as if there was nothing unusual about standing on the beach with two soaked, bloodstained doctors. 'It's good to meet you at last. Your husband's told me all about you.'

'He's not my husband,' Anya said shortly.

'No? Sorry.' Despite his urbanity, the guy was clearly distracted. 'Joe tells me you did great. We'll have a drink later, but not now. There's so much…'

He hesitated and then grimaced. 'First things first. Troy and Nathan are part of the film crew, here to shoot the latest Gerry Boyne thriller. When news gets out I'll have every media outlet trying to get on the island, and the last thing I want is aerial shots that look as gruesome as this.' He motioned to the staff trying to haul the wreck of the jet-skis to shore, and to the bloodstained gear still on the beach. 'Ugh.'

'Does that include us?' Ben queried, and Martin had the grace to give an apologetic smile.

'If you wouldn't mind…'

'We're clearing off,' Ben told him. 'But Martin, first thing…that was a disaster that could have been avoided. Those men were so drunk it made medical treatment almost impossible. So our first condition as incoming resort doctors is that no guest gets on a recreational motorised vehicle without a breath test. Starting now.'

Martin stared at him for a long moment, seemingly considering, but then shook his head.

'There's no way we can refuse what the super-stars want—but I will ask the staff to give warn-ings.'

'No warnings. Just the rule.'

'Look, I don't have time to talk about this now.'

Ben's face hardened. 'A rule or we leave—and we tell the media why we're leaving.'

Simple as that.

'Ben...'

'Those guys almost killed each other,' Ben said harshly. 'And it could have been worse. They were using jet-skis in the swimming area, in shallow water. Your lifeguards didn't seem to have any control. They could have slammed into kids, into other guests, or maybe into the dolphins out there, which would have upset ev-eryone who saw. This is non-negotiable, mate. Take it or leave it.'

The men stared at each other. This was a side of Ben that Anya hadn't seen before, uncompro-mising, grim—ready to walk away.

Walk her away? This was her job too. But she was already moving closer to Ben, facing Martin down as well. They might not be married but in this they were a partnership. As one.

'We'll talk about it later,' Martin tried.

'Now. Or we walk. This whole mess was avoidable.'

'You can't leave.'

'So make the decision.'

Finally the man shrugged. 'Fine,' he said, almost pettishly. 'Will you talk to the press, after you've cleaned up, of course? They'll want to know the extent of the injuries.'

'Tell them to contact the hospital in Cairns,' Ben said. 'I can't imagine you'll want us to release confidential patient information.'

The man's face paled. 'No!' he muttered. 'Of all the things to happen… This could well crash the resort if they shift the blame to us.'

'You might,' Ben suggested diffidently, 'like to send a report to the mainland police, with a possible suggestion. Driving water craft when intoxicated is illegal, isn't it? National laws are national laws, and people are responsible for their own behaviour. The doctors in Cairns will do blood tests if the police request it. I'll write suspected intoxication in a report if you wish.'

There was a moment's silence and then Martin's face cleared. 'Good. I'll do that. Dammit, I can't let the movie lot blame us.' His panic seemed to ease and he regarded them almost benignly. 'You're heading off now?'

'We're taking our disgusting selves out of sight of any marauding cameras,' Ben said promptly. 'Come on, Anya. Let's go.'

They walked back to their bungalow in silence, each intent on their own thoughts. But Anya got halfway there and had to stop. She was shaking, she realised. The adrenalin of the catastrophe had dissipated and shock was setting in.

She was a competent doctor, she'd coped with emergency situations in the past, but never before had she come so close to losing a life in such circumstances.

She was filthy. Her body was still sticky with dried blood. She was wearing someone else's dumb Hawaiian shirt and even that was blood-stained.

Suddenly her body didn't want to move.

'Give me a minute,' she said, standing still and taking deep breaths. If she didn't know better she'd say she was heading for a panic attack—but surely doctors didn't have panic attacks. The two women on the beach, girlfriends of the guys who'd been airlifted to Brisbane, had both had full-blown ones and they'd been distractions she and Ben could have done without.

She stood absolutely still, she focused on breathing and waited for this to pass.

Ben stood back and waited. He stayed by her side, a tiny bit distant, with her but not. Giving her space. She was aware that he was there, she was almost grateful for his presence, but she needed to focus only on herself.

Breathe, breathe, breathe...

And finally it eased. The sense of overwhelming catastrophe, the feeling that the world was crushing her, that she was totally out of control, there was nothing she could do, nowhere she could go, finally it backed off. She let it subside a little more and then sighed.

'Sorry,' she muttered, and Ben's voice answered gently.

'Don't be. You did great, Dr Greer.'

'Yeah, but...'

'No buts.' He reached out and took her hand in his, his fingers laced through hers, and there was the gentlest of pressure. 'Your mum died six weeks back, your fiancé turned out to be a louse, you've packed up your home and you've travelled to another state, another job. This afternoon you saved a guy from bleeding out, all the while stopping him from drowning. You want to take twenty-four hours to focus on your breathing, that's okay by me. Totally justifiable.'

She nodded. Said like that, it put things in perspective.

'You did a great job too,' she ventured. 'You want to breathe a little as well?'

'I'd rather have a shower.' He tugged her round so she was facing the path. 'Good idea?'

'Yeah.' But as his hand tugged her forward, as they headed for the bungalow again, the memory of his words to Martin started replaying in her mind. His anger had almost matched her panic attack, she thought, and she knew that if Martin hadn't caved he would have left the island. Right now.

'Ben,' she said carefully into the stillness. They were walking again, hand in hand. It was a strange sensation of familiarity, but it felt okay.

More than okay. It felt right.

'Yep?' They were speeding up now, in the home stretch, hot showers beckoning like a siren song.

'When you told me your wife was killed in an accident…was that caused by a drunk driver?'

'Yes,' he said shortly, and his hand was withdrawn as if she'd stuck something sharp into his palm.

'I'm sorry. It's none of my business. I just thought…it did seem personal back there.'

'A bloody waste,' he muttered. 'Two guys who're going to regret this day for the rest of their lives.'

'At least they did it to themselves, not to others,' she ventured. 'If they'd crashed into swimmers…'

'That would have been much worse.' But there was something in his voice—it was loaded with bitterness? She cast a curious glance at him, her own shock and nerves subsiding into the background.

Should she shut up? She didn't. Maybe it was her medical training—ask the hard questions, you'll never figure what's really wrong if you don't ask. Like asking someone who seemed depressed or too quiet or maybe agitated, 'Are you thinking of suicide?' She'd been trained always to ask.

Maybe that was the reason she opened her mouth again.

'A drunken driver killing your wife, injuring you so badly…is today bringing that back for you?'

There was another silence then, a long one. Maybe he wouldn't answer, she thought. They walked on but as they neared the bungalow he paused.

'You go ahead,' he told her. 'Two people using the hot water at the same time'll probably strain the system anyway. I need to walk things off. I'll head up to Reception and do that report for Martin.'

'In those clothes?'

'I assume they have a back door. And the worst has already washed off.'

'You're not exactly respectable,' she told him and then paused. 'Ben, is there any way I can help?'

'No,' he said shortly and then he exhaled.

'You can't,' he told her. 'It's just…a drunken driver did kill Rihanna and injure me. Only that drunken driver was Rihanna.'

CHAPTER SEVEN

WHY HAD HE told her that?

Left with his thoughts, they weren't exactly comforting. It felt almost a betrayal.

He'd told no one.

The speed. The white lines blurring in front of him. His voice, demanding Rihanna slow down…

After that, a merciful blank.

But he'd woken after a few days to pain, to endless medical treatment, to never-ending sympathy and kindness. He'd been surrounded by eulogies for a beloved wife and daughter, a woman who, according to the police, could have ended up driving straight into the path of an oncoming car.

A burly police sergeant had come to see him in hospital, driven by, what, sympathy?

'Mate, there's CCTV along that stretch of road. Your car was turning into that bend way too fast, and in the end it looked to be heading straight for the other sedan. Mum and Dad and three little kiddies were in that car. Now, I dunno for sure what happened, but the view on the CCTV looked pretty clear—you seemed to lean over and wrench the wheel. You hit a tree instead of the oncoming car. Mate, if you're prepared to let people know just how drunk your wife was, I'd be backing you. In my book you're a bloody hero.'

A hero. Great. What was the use of that? No. Let people think Rihanna was the angelic wife and mother the eulogy said she was.

But he would get the Breath Test Before Use rule enforced on the beach. Anya would back him up, he knew she would. And why was he thinking of this now, of Rihanna, of his marriage, of a time he desperately wanted to put behind him?

Because of the blood, the chaos, the fear of this afternoon, he thought. He'd been away from medicine for so long. Was this post-traumatic stress? Was one accident making him think of another?

Or was it Anya, looking ghastly in her blood-stained borrowed clothes? Anya, coping with chaos, waiting until it was all over to allow herself the luxury of personal reaction. Anya… Was she what a real hero should look like?

Yes, it was, he thought, and his pacing feet slowed. Anya, who'd be back in the bungalow now, showering—in what should have been their en suite bathroom but was now firmly labelled *her* bathroom.

Was she shaking again?

What was he doing, walking aimlessly around the island when Anya might be needing him?

Anya didn't need him. He thought of those two wardrobes and he found himself grinning. He knew deep down that the reaction that had made her cling to him, that had let him grasp her hand, that had forced her to hold it as if it was there to save her, was an aberration.

Anya. One strong woman.

Wardrobes. Two separate beds.

They were now colleagues. There was a whole new future to think about.

Um…think about what? She was still in the midst of shock and grief. Back away, he told himself, but even as he did he was turning back to the bungalow.

Home? Back to Anya?

She'd be in the shower. He could imagine her there, maybe shaking again as the events of the afternoon replayed in her head.

She was his colleague. He needed to support her.

Yes, he needed to go home.

She stood under the shower for a long, long time, and it was wonderful. The bungalow's 'en suite' was so much more than just a bathroom. The tiny courtyard was netted overhead to keep the bugs at bay, but it looked almost like a slice of rainforest. Its floor was made of roughly hewn stone and its walls were covered with some sort of flowering vine—mandevilla?—a mass of deep pink, pale pink and white blooms. Palms leaned overhead and the squawks of lorikeets made her feel as if she were almost in a menagerie.

Along the edges of the stone floor, out of range of hot water but close enough to enjoy the steam, she could see at least half a dozen bright green tree frogs. The sweet-smelling soaps and hair products lined up for use had discreet labels— 'not harmful for wildlife'—and the frogs looked as if they were even enjoying them.

This was okay. More than okay.

She stood under the stream of luscious warm water, she used meditation techniques she'd learned during medical training to let the nightmare of the afternoon dissipate and she let herself think that this job…might even be good. This afternoon's drama had taught her that she and Ben were needed, but such incidents must surely be rare. The job must be as promised. Rich tourists doing stupid things, patients who'd be evacuated if they needed real medical help, this place…

Ben.

The thought of him cut into her deliberately

peaceful thoughts. Ben. She'd thought she was escaping emotional ties by coming to Dolphin Island. What she'd learned today was that Ben had just as much emotional baggage as she did.

No, she thought fairly. More. She'd lost her mum, but her mum's health had been precarious and they'd both known her time was limited. And somehow she'd escaped from a marriage that, looking at it in hindsight after a whole six weeks, she knew would have been disastrous if it had gone ahead.

A door banged from outside and she heard footsteps treading across the wooden floor. She thought of Ben, going to his side of the bedroom, collecting what he needed, heading to the small bathroom off the living room. A plain, ordinary bathroom, not the tropical splendour she was savouring.

'He deserves no less,' she told the frogs who were sitting on their respective rocks, savouring the steam she was creating. 'Letting people even think we're a couple.'

And then the water pressure dipped a bit and she thought, Fair's fair. She'd had a gorgeous soak, her head was together again, and Ben deserved as much water pressure as she could give him.

And more. On the beach… The tracheostomy… 'I don't think I could have done it,' she told the frogs. Now the stream of hot water had ceased, they were off their rocks and hopping through the puddles on the shower room floor.

'You could get trodden on,' she told them, but she was suddenly no longer thinking about frogs. Her mind had been caught by the vision of Ben in his own shower. That long, lithe body, water streaming down his back, his hair slick and wet, his eyes closed, maybe lifting his arms to savour the sensation.

Naked. Ben.

'Well, that goes to show how shattered you are at losing Mathew,' she said, speaking to herself now and speaking sternly. 'Or not. Out of the frying pan, into the fire? I don't think so. Don't even think about going there.'

And with that she wrapped one of the resort's luscious towels around her body and headed back to her bedroom. *Their* bedroom?

She dressed fast, conscious that Ben could finish in the shower soon—he'd have no frogs to play with. It didn't matter if he came in, she told herself. The rooms were well divided, and she was on the far side. Nevertheless, she dressed fast, donning a crop top and sarong—two things she'd bought on a whim from the airport shop. Okay, she thought, staring at herself in the mirror. Surely now it's time for a piña colada. Or even two.

Almost as she thought it, she heard Ben walk into his side of the bedroom.

And then she heard a knock on the outside door.

It was actually quite hard to answer the door. She needed to walk past Ben's side of the bedroom to get there.

'Are you respectable?' she called, feeling silly.

'Always respectable,' he called back, and she metaphorically girded her loins and marched past. Eyes straight in front.

Maybe only a tiny glance to the left to see a bare chest being towelled dry.

Dear heaven, that body was hot.

'Says the devastated bride,' she muttered to herself and, thrusting aside the desire to take a longer glance, she marched to the door and opened it.

A woman was standing under the porch. She looked very like the two women who'd been screaming on the beach as their boyfriends were being treated. Another of the movie set? Sleek, blonde, gorgeous, the woman was manicured and made-up to within an inch of her life, and from the moment she opened her mouth she oozed entitlement.

'Is the doctor here?' Her tone pretty much said, Stand aside, servant, lead me to someone important.

'I'm a doctor,' Anya said mildly, and the woman blinked in disbelief.

'They said it was a man. Dr Duncan.'

'That would be me.' And Ben was behind her, naked except for a towel draped round his waist.

The woman took a step back. 'You don't look like doctors.' It was an accusation.

'Whoops,' Ben said and smiled and turned to the medical kit which had been lugged back from the beach and dumped inside the door. He reached down—dangerous when his towel didn't look all that securely fastened, grabbed a stethoscope and fastened it round his neck. 'Is this better?'

'We really are doctors,' Anya said quickly, frowning him down. 'Just in off-duty clothes. How can we help?'

'My…my boyfriend.'

'Is he ill?'

'Yeah. He keeps moaning. He got a bit sunburned today and you'd think he'd been dipped in hot oil, the fuss he's making. Not,' she added quickly. 'that he's not entitled to make a fuss. He's Ricardo de Silva.'

She obviously expected them to know the name, and Anya did. Ricardo de Silva was the latest media sensation, a hot young movie star. He'd obviously be on the island for the making of the film.

'Can you ask him to come to the clinic?' she

said, casting a dubious glance next door. Neither she nor Ben had had a chance to check the clinic out yet, but she assumed there were facilities.

But the woman had stiffened. 'You come to him,' she said, sounding shocked. 'He's ill. The contract says twenty-four-hour medical care. You can't expect him to walk over here.'

'Which bungalow are you in?' Ben asked before she could respond.

'Number one,' the woman said, as if it was obvious. 'The one with its own horizon pool. And hurry. I don't know why I had to come myself, there was no one answering on Reception.'

'I guess they're busy,' Anya said, figuring she might do a bit of damage control on the island's behalf. 'Every media outlet in Australia and a whole lot overseas will be searching for news about this afternoon's accident.'

'Look, I don't care about them,' the woman said hotly. 'They're not stars. Ricardo needs attention now. Are you coming or not?'

'Give us five minutes,' Ben said. 'Sunburn, you think. I gather you think he'll survive that long?'

'Don't be funny,' she snapped and turned on her heel and stalked away.

'I can do this myself,' she told Ben as they watched the woman depart. He surely didn't look like an efficient, clinical doctor.

'Um…look at yourself,' he told her. 'Sarong? Crop top? Do you know this guy's reputation? How tightly tied is that sarong?'

'Don't be ridiculous. He's got a girlfriend.'

'Reports are it's never stopped him in the past.'

'Well, reports are that you're as likely to be at risk as I am,' she retorted. 'And your towel looks more precarious than my sarong.'

He grinned. 'I reckon we're okay. There's nothing like a little sunburn to dampen testosterone.'

'A little sunburn?' She assumed mock outrage. 'Didn't you hear the woman? He's in agony.'

'Then let's go see if we can fix the agony. You reckon we should don full theatre gear?'

'Not a snowball's chance in a bushfire,' she said briskly. 'I have a piña colada with my name on it waiting in the bar, and His Lordship's bungalow is almost in a direct line.'

'And I'm thinking there might be a hamburger attached to said piña colada. I'm starving. Okay, let's go treat a sunburn fast—though maybe we should put on clothes that look a bit more professional.'

'What, take this job seriously, you mean?'

'I guess,' he said reluctantly. 'But I'm starting to worry. This job seems to be getting in the way of its job description.'

They did change, into decent trousers and shirt and demure trousers and blouse respectively, but as they walked down towards the beach their mood was strangely lighter. Ben had put together a bag of what they might need, and the walk through the discreetly lit, ever so carefully natural, bush path towards the movie star's bungalow was a lovely one. Ben's limp was a little more pronounced than usual—it had been quite some day.

This afternoon had been as shocking a scene as Anya had ever encountered, she thought. It wasn't only that Ben's leg was giving him trouble. She was also having trouble keeping her thoughts under control. The adrenalin, her emotion afterwards, Ben's frank admission of his wife's death, they'd left her reeling.

So break the moment.

Time and time again after drama, medics could be found reacting with a humour that outsiders sometimes found shocking. But it worked. Often humour could break the appalling tension of what had gone before.

So try.

'You know,' she said thoughtfully as they walked under the palms in the warm dusk breeze, 'this is a great spot for drop bears.'

The legendary and entirely mythical Australian drop bear had been referred to since time immemorial to scare newcomers in this type of situation. The story was that the bears hung high in just such places, only to drop when least expected on the unwary folk underneath. And suddenly she had an urge to share her own drop bear story with Ben.

'You can't scare me with drop bears,' Ben told her, smiling. 'I was brought up on drop bear stories.'

She grinned. 'Rats. But here's a story. My mum told me that Dad terrified her as a new bride. He ended up carrying her all the way home from the local pub "in order to protect her from the bears". "It was the most romantic thing," Mum told me, and she giggled every time she thought about it. I think she was almost disappointed when she found out they didn't exist.'

Ben chuckled—and the deep chuckle sounded good. The tension of the day dissipated still further.

'So are you absolutely sure they don't exist?' she asked Ben. 'You know, if you don't believe in them it's been statistically proven you have a seventy-nine percent higher chance of being dropped on.' She had a sudden ridiculous vision of her picking him up and lugging him home. And the thought made *her* giggle.

'What?' he demanded, and she told him and he grinned.

'I'd like to see you try.'

'Hey, I've chopped wood since I was ten years old. Arms like oaks.'

'Try it,' he said and stopped dead and spread his arms, willing for her to lift.

'If a drop bear descends, I will,' she said with dignity. 'So are you absolutely sure they're not here?'

'Impossible,' he said firmly. 'I've been through the items we can claim for government rebate on this island, and bites and bruises from drop bears doesn't appear once. Though,' he said thoughtfully, 'I can't say Martin won't have collared every drop bear and had them held captive at the far end of the island, in order to keep his precious film crew safe.'

She chuckled, but medicine had to intrude again. They'd reached the bungalow—if it could be called that. This was a more impressive building than anything they'd seen on the island, a mini mansion set right on the beach. The lights were on over massive Balinese-style doors and when Ben lifted the huge knocker and let it fall, the thud on the thick wood—complete with echo—made Anya start.

And then she pretty much jumped again. The guy who opened the door was huge. He was wearing black jeans, black T-shirt, black sunglasses, his arms were like tree trunks and his neck…well, gorilla sprang to mind as a comparison. He was also wearing the sort of welcoming expression a gorilla might be proud of.

'Yeah?' It was a deep, guttural growl, a warning all on its own.

'We're the doctors, here to see Mr de Silva.'

'You don't look like doctors.' So much for their neat clothes, Anya thought. What did he want, white coats?

'They are.' The girl appeared in the background, sounding sulky. 'Let 'em in, Rod.'

'You sure?'

'They're all this crappy island has,' she snapped, and led the way into the living room.

Ricardo de Silva was lying stretched out on a vast leopard-skin couch and he was everything a movie star should be. Anya stopped in the doorway, stunned, and only Ben prodding her in the small of her back made her recover.

The movie star looked…amazing. He was tanned to a deep, deep gold, his shoulder-length blond hair was tumbling to his shoulders and he was naked, apart from what looked to be little more than a loincloth. He looked up at them with startling blue eyes and a mouth already pursed in anger.

'You took your time,' he snarled. 'I'm in pain here. I need some decent drugs, and fast. And why do I need two of you?'

'We're a partnership,' Ben said smoothly, but Anya heard a faint tremor in his voice. This set-up was ludicrous, almost comical. The gorilla bodyguard, the manicured beauty, the he-

man alpha hero, lying on his faux fur settee...
It looked like a movie scene all by itself. 'We
work together. Your...partner...tells me you're
sunburned.'

'She's not my partner,' he growled, scowling
at the unfortunate woman. 'Mia's an idiot. Why
didn't she get burned? I told her to get sun stuff
and whatever she used, it didn't work.'

'Honey, it was coconut oil,' the unfortunate
Mia wailed. 'When you're as tanned as we are,
you don't need kids-type sunscreen.'

Uh-oh. Anya edged a little closer to the man
on the sofa. He certainly looked tanned—but
was that inflammation underneath?

'Is that tan real?' Ben asked conversationally,
and Ricardo flashed him a look of pure filth.
'Piss off.'

'Maybe we could ask your bodyguard and
your...friend to leave for a moment,' Ben said
smoothly. 'If we're to examine...'

'We're going,' the woman said hastily and
practically pushed the gorilla out of the door,
slamming it behind them.

Leaving Ben and Anya looking down at their
patient.

'You have blisters on your shoulders,' Anya
said, softly now and sympathetically. This really did look painful. 'How long were you out
in the sun?'

'Most of the day.' He glowered. 'We were supposed to have the day off and then do a dusk and night scene tonight. So we caught some rays.'

'You surely did.'

'I told her to bring the lotion,' he growled. 'Stupid b…'

'Did you specify sunscreen?' Ben said mildly. 'Fifty plus protection? Waterproof?'

'She should have known.'

'If she has brown skin already and has a decent natural tan, she might think you just wanted to get darker,' Ben said. 'The tan…it's fake, isn't it?' He too had walked forward.

And winced.

From the door the man had looked absurdly, impossibly handsome—impossibly tanned—but up close the tan was underlaid by vicious red. All over. There were blisters on his shoulders and his stomach. Were there blisters on his head?

'Could I check?' Ben asked.

'Don't you dare hurt me.'

'I won't,' Ben said but he tentatively lifted a lock of the blond hair.

The scalp underneath was red as well.

'No hat?' he asked mildly.

'It must have come off.' It was a sullen mutter. 'And I told you, she was supposed to cream me up.'

'Does she know how fair-skinned you really are?'

There was no answer.

'How are you feeling?' Ben asked. 'Headache? Any dizziness?'

'Just damn pain.'

'That's reassuring,' Ben told him. 'I know the pain's an issue but you're lucky to have avoided a major case of sunstroke. There are a few things that'll help. First is to drink fluids, lots of fluids. A cool bath will help—you might need to hop in and out a few times overnight when you feel your body overheating. There's a king-sized tub of aloe vera in our kit—sunburn is something seen a lot in this climate. Lather it on everywhere, it really does work. Then anti-inflammatories, aspirin's probably the best. Do you have any, or will we leave you some?'

'I don't want blasted aspirin. I want something with grunt. Morphine. This pain's crazy.'

'Have you had morphine before?' Ben asked mildly and Anya nodded silently to herself. The way he'd asked for morphine…

'Just for damn pain.'

'Do you have any on hand now?'

'I'm out,' the guy said sulkily. 'Sore throat last week. I can't work with a sore throat.'

'Could you give me the contact details of the doctor who prescribed you the last lot?'

There was a moment's stillness and then the guy's eyes narrowed. 'You think I'm an addict.'

'I don't,' Ben said quietly. 'But morphine for a sore throat, morphine for sunburn when I don't know you? I can't in good faith prescribe you any tonight. Aspirin, aloe vera and cold baths…'

'What the…? Mia!' he roared and as the woman reappeared, looking scared, he yelled, 'Get me the island manager. Get me Sven!'

'Sven's caught up with the fuss from the two guys who were hurt this afternoon,' Mia said apologetically. 'Sven's our director,' she explained to Ben, her eyes not leaving Ricardo's face. 'And he's up to his ears, trying to figure how to shoot tomorrow without Troy and Nathan.'

'That's unfortunate,' Ben said sympathetically. 'But now there might be more trouble. Aloe vera and aspirin will cope with the pain, but you're going to peel,' he told Ricardo. 'All over. The skin underneath will be raw. I'd advise no cosmetics until you completely heal. Your tan's going to disappear too,' he added. 'You might need to make plans.'

'What the…? Fix it!' the man screamed, and Ben turned to Mia.

'We're leaving you anti-inflammatories and aloe vera,' he told her, 'but that's all we can do. I'm sorry but you seem to be in for an uncomfortable night.' And the look he gave her was one of pure sympathy.

'You can't just leave!' Ricardo yelled, but Ben shook his head.

'There's nothing else we can do. Do you concur, Dr Greer?'

'Absolutely,' Anya said unsteadily, taking one last look at the ridiculous setting—and at the panic in the eyes of the unfortunate Mia. And then she hesitated, glancing across at Ricardo and then back at the woman.

And Ben got it almost before she did.

'Mia, if you need anything else for yourself, any support, we're available twenty-four-seven,' he said, watching the girl's face.

'What, if he hits me, do you mean?'

Bang. She hadn't imagined it then, that flash of fear, and Ben had obviously seen it too.

'I can't imagine that will happen,' Ben said smoothly, and he gave Ricardo a long, considering stare. 'But Mia, you know where we are, and the resort's security guys are always on hand.'

'I'm not going to hit her!' Ricardo roared.

'I'm sure you won't,' Ben said.

She hadn't been aware that she'd been holding her breath, but it was released in a rush. Now that it had been said out loud, now the guy knew Ben was wary, she was pretty sure there'd be no physical assault.

'Mia, we'll contact you in the morning and see how things are going,' Ben was saying. 'Now, if you'll excuse us, Dr Greer and I have another urgent case to attend.'

'I… I will come to see you tomorrow, if that's

all right,' Mia muttered, with another nervous glance at her boyfriend. 'Just…just to let you know how Ricardo is.'

'That'll be fine,' Anya told her, taking up Ben's cues. 'I'll book you in for a consultation at nine.'

CHAPTER EIGHT

THEY LEFT, THEIR steps automatically turning towards the bar.

'Urgent case?' Anya said once they were out of earshot of the goon watching them go from the bungalow's portico.

'Malnutrition plus dehydration,' he said. 'And urgent's too mild a description.

'Symptoms?'

'Extreme crabbiness. This job was supposed to be a walk in the park. We appear to be working overtime already. Though we do appear to have done good.'

'Treating sunburn?'

'We did save two lives. Plus,' he added softly, 'I suspect we've stopped a woman being bashed tonight.'

'You guessed. Good call, Dr Duncan.'

'I saw your face. You guessed it, too. I'm willing to bet you'll have her in the clinic tomorrow, weeping buckets.'

'I hope I do,' she said, her voice softening.

'What a toerag. She might be the epitome of dumb blonde, but to treat her like that...'

'Will you advise her to go home?'

'The whole movie crowd might go home,' she said thoughtfully. 'They've lost two minor actors and now, having a leading man who's alternately itching, peeling and swearing... Problematic, wouldn't you say?'

'Martin's not going to thank us when we break the news.'

'He's not, is he?' she said, suddenly cheerful again. They'd almost reached the bar and she could smell food. Was that fried onions? 'And you know the one great thing about today?'

'What's that?' He was watching her, a curious look on his face. As if he didn't quite get her.

Maybe she had no reason to be smiling, she thought, but suddenly she couldn't help it. Yes, the day had been horrific, but she'd been a doctor for long enough to know she could normally block things out. A hamburger with crispy bun oozing with butter and fried onions was surely therapy of the best kind, and *surely* it was time for her piña colada now?

And this place was fabulous. The twinkling lights over the vast veranda of the bar. The soft wash of the tiny waves on the nearby beach. The moonlight over the water...

And added to that...the thing that made her smile most...

'You know,' she said, her smile getting wider. 'We've worked our butts off today, Dr Duncan, and no one, not one single person, has said thank you.'

'They won't either,' Ben said morosely. 'We've stuffed their movie.'

'Not us, Dick the Duck,' she said lightly. They'd arrived at the terrace and a waiter was coming forward to greet them—and surely that was a drinks menu in his hand. 'They did it all by themselves. Not a thank you in sight, and here comes my piña colada. Welcome to our brand-new world, Dr Duncan. Let's dive straight in.'

They were late to the bar. The movie crowd, who, they were told, represented almost half the island's guests, was noticeably absent. Maybe they were too shocked to be out drinking in such a public place or maybe they were gathered somewhere changing plans. After the news of Ricardo broke, there'd be an even greater need to replan.

There was thus a minimal wait on service. Ten minutes after they arrived they were sitting in gorgeous, plushly cushioned cane armchairs, wrapping themselves around hamburgers that were everything Anya could wish for. There was also a piña colada for Anya and a large, ice-cold beer for Ben. Anya finished her cocktail fast—and then looked regretfully at the empty glass.

'Go on,' Ben told her, grinning. 'I'll be the on-call doctor tonight.'

'There'd better not be another call,' she told him. 'Being busy seems a serious breach of our contract.'

Then Martin arrived with a man and a woman they hadn't met before, all of them looking practically bug-eyed.

'What's this I hear about Ricardo?' Martin demanded. 'Sunburn? His girlfriend's been onto Sven here saying he won't be able to work. Surely you can fix sunburn?' His tone was pure challenge.

'We don't have to,' Ben said mildly. 'It'll fix itself. He's been lucky to escape sunstroke. He'll be itchy for a while but he's okay.'

'But he says he'll peel!' The plump little man beside him—introduced as Sven, the film director—was looking as if he was about to have kittens. 'And Serena here says she can't do make-up on sunburned skin.'

'It would look awful,' the woman said. Martin's introduction had been sketchy—'This is Serena, our make-up artist'—and it was clear both regarded her as a minion. 'But there are worse problems. If the skin's peeling...'

'There must be a way,' Sven snapped.

'The make-up will peel off with the skin,' Serena said miserably. 'Unless I cake it so thick it can't look natural.'

'If you put thick make-up on skin so severely sunburned you run an almost certain risk of infection,' Ben told them.

'But he's essential,' Sven snapped. 'Sunburn! It's nothing. Surely we can manage. I can get by without two yahoos this afternoon, but not Ricardo.'

It seemed major injury to two actors was a minor inconvenience, but the effect of sunburn was a potential disaster. There was a moment's silence while Anya and Ben mutually and silently decided to let that go through to the keeper.

'So you'd be prepared to risk someone as high profile as Ricardo getting a major infection on your watch?' Ben asked at last.

'There are antibiotics…'

'We strongly advise against it,' he said flatly. The realisation that, for this man, the two severely injured actors were of no account in the face of a case of sunburn had turned Ben's attitude to grim. 'And I'm afraid it'll need to be written up in the medical notes, there for possible legal subpoena. That's all we can say.'

'But…'

'I'm sorry but my hamburger's getting cold,' Anya interjected as her second piña colada arrived. She really was hungry. 'Would you mind if we eat?'

She got a glower from both Martin and Sven, and a shy smile from the make-up artist.

'Go right ahead,' Martin snapped—and the party retreated.

Anya munched on her burger and watched them go, her expression speculative.

'You realise you just annoyed our boss,' Ben said, but he was watching her with a faint twinkle in his eyes.

'Couldn't be helped.' She was on her third bite. 'This is delicious!'

'You could be sacked.'

'And I just figured that I don't care. There are other tropical islands. They're not grateful to me and I'm not grateful to them. I can walk away in a heartbeat. How good is that?'

'It's not bad at all,' Ben said slowly, watching her turn her attention back to her piña colada.

'These have to be the best piña coladas I've ever had,' she said happily. 'Not that I've had many. Maybe two max, until now. Are you sure you don't want one?'

'One of us needs to stay sober tonight. Professional ethics.'

'Then I'm glad it's you,' she told him. 'And I swear I won't even say thank you.'

For all she'd intended to make a night of it, it didn't happen. Hamburger consumed, halfway into her second cocktail weariness hit like a tsunami. One moment she was high on the adrenalin of this afternoon's rescue, the ridiculousness of the night's sunburn victim, the realisation that she could walk away with no compunction if anyone wanted to sack her. The next it was almost too much effort to raise her glass.

She put her glass down on the table and noticed, with some annoyance, that her hand was suddenly shaking.

'Had enough?' Ben asked mildly, and she flashed him a look of annoyance. That was the type of comment Mathew would have made.

'I can drink more if I want to.'

'I wasn't talking about alcohol. I was talking about you. Today. These past weeks. This whole set-up.'

She looked at him uncertainly, not sure whether to take offence or not. But his eyes were kind.

As Mathew's had been, she thought, but Mathew being *kind* was different. Mathew being *kind* was smothering. Mathew thought he knew what was best for her.

The whole town had thought they knew what was best for Anya and her mother.

Why was she thinking about that now? Why was she suddenly feeling…odd?

'I guess I have had enough of today,' she said, but her mind was still intent on this puzzle. Why did it feel so different, the way this man asked how she was feeling? 'I… It's probably time for bed,' she managed but her sense of confusion was growing.

'I might be headed that way too,' he told her in a voice that said her decision was just that— *her* decision. 'It didn't do my back or leg any good at all, hauling an idiot out from under a jet-ski. What I really need right now is a massage. I bet there are scores of masseurs on this island. Should I ring for room service? How do you think that'd go down?'

And that made her grin. 'So…the new doctor on the island would be calling for the island masseur at midnight on his first day on the job…'

'Hardly a good look?'

She chuckled. 'Possibly not.'

But… *I could give you a massage.* The thought was there in her head, almost bursting to be said out loud. She'd done a massage course. Her mother had had arthritis along with everything else, and she'd loved doing that for her. She was actually pretty good.

But not here. Not with this man. Despite her weariness, alarms were sounding all over the place.

'You'll just have to sleep it off,' she said instead, and pushed the remains of her cocktail aside. 'Bedtime for the island doctors.'

'For the new roomies,' he said and rose and held out a hand to help her up. 'I hope you don't snore.'

'The feeling's mutual, Dr Duncan,' she told him. 'But, even if you do, I reckon sleep is only minutes away.'

Except it wasn't. They walked home in silence, but it wasn't a comfortable silence. Something had happened.

The day had happened. Last-minute packing. Frantic goodbyes. Janet driving her to Sydney and then a flight to Cairns. The ferry ride to the island, cruising across the breathtaking waters of Australia's Great Barrier Reef. Being transported from one world to another. She'd walked—or rushed—out of the world she knew, and suddenly she was a doctor in surely one of the most beautiful places on earth.

Then there'd been the shock of the shared house, the discussion of pretend marriage, the unnerving knowledge that she'd be sleeping metres from this man, with not even a wall between them. But she'd not even had time to let that sink in before they'd been thrown into a life-threatening medical trauma.

That had made her realise just how good Ben was—how skilled. She'd spent so little time with him back in Merriwood that, apart from the fast Caesarean, she hadn't had time to properly assess his medical skills. But she'd thought there'd be little use for extensive medical skills here.

One afternoon had taught her how wrong that

thought had been, and one afternoon had shown her the breadth of Ben's abilities. What he'd done on the beach… The memory of it still took her breath away.

Then there was the gut-lurch when he'd told her about his wife. She'd been trying to block it out—it was surely none of her business—but it refused to be blocked. It had stayed in the back of her mind during the stupidity of the sunburn incident. While she'd seen the way he'd handled it. His…kindness? Wrong word maybe.

Mathew had been kind. Ben was nothing like Mathew.

She was suddenly—and inappropriately—thinking of the way he'd smiled at her over the table as she'd tackled her hamburger and her cocktail.

Her two cocktails, she corrected herself. It was no wonder she was feeling a bit…fuzzy. Warm.

Why was his hand holding hers?

How had that happened? He'd held out a hand to help her from the table—she remembered that—and then the steps down from the terrace had been dimly lit, and he certainly wouldn't want his medical partner falling.

He was using a cane. She should be taking his hand.

Well, she was holding it, she told herself. Maybe that was how it had happened. Maybe his injured leg was the reason she wasn't pulling away.

Liar, liar, pants on fire.

'Tell me about your wife,' she asked suddenly and a bit too fast. Why had she asked? To break this sense of intimacy? To find out more about this man who was holding her hand? It was definitely none of her business, she had no right to ask, but the question was out there now.

He stopped walking. The question hung, waiting for an answer.

It didn't get one.

'I'm sorry.' She broke the silence, speaking a bit too fast. 'Ben... I had no business asking. It was just...'

'That I told you about Rihanna's drinking?'

'I guess, but I had no right. It just...came out. I'm sorry,' she repeated.

'There's no need to be sorry.' Their linked hands had somehow disconnected. He stood in the dim light, leaning heavily on his cane and his voice was heavy to match.

'Just don't see me as a grieving widower,' he said at last. 'I wasn't much more than a kid when I met Rihanna. I was a med student with my head in my books. Rihanna had just got a job as a junior television presenter and she was so glamorous. She was also intent on one thing—promoting Rihanna—but of course I didn't see that.'

That was followed by a long pause. Anya tried to think of something to say and then decided nothing was the only option. Finally, he seemed to force himself to continue.

'Anyway, we dated for a few months—I thought fairly casually—and then she fell pregnant. At least she told me she was pregnant. And I know this sounds callous but, looking back, I don't know what to believe. Rihanna… Well, my parents are old money, part of the Sydney *Who's Who*, with all the right connections. They're also incredibly social, and Rihanna loved being part of that. I didn't realise how much until…after. Anyway, there was no baby. Our marriage was empty almost from the start, and when she died she was pregnant to another man.'

'Oh, Ben…'

'Don't you dare say you're sorry,' he said, savagely now. 'I've had enough sympathy to last a lifetime. Like your gratitude, I've had enough.'

Whoa.

Where to go from here? She took a deep breath and tried to get her thoughts in order. They wouldn't…order. She thought suddenly of the tissue box she kept in her consulting rooms. A big one. Sometimes she needed to hand over tissues and delve into a patient's grief. Sometimes it was better to retreat and be practical.

Right now, tissues didn't seem the way to go.

'Well,' she said at last, 'I thought *I* needed a

tropical island and piña coladas. I reckon your need is double, yet you ordered only a single beer tonight! Surely you can do better than that. What's the saying? Physician, heal thyself. You need to pull your act together.'

And to her relief he gave a grunt of something that could almost have been laughter. 'You're prescribing *me* piña coladas?'

'If you won't prescribe them for yourself then someone should. Plus as much self-indulgence as you can manage—this job really does need to be a doddle.'

'It does, doesn't it?' he said, and his smile re-appeared. There was a moment's pause while he seemed to gather himself back into the persona he presented to the world. Physician in charge of his world? 'Meanwhile, let's go home.' And his hand reached out and caught hers again.

The linking was a relief. It eased things. It helped…her as well as him? They walked on, slowly, in deference to his stiff leg—but also slowly because her thoughts were whirling—and maybe his too. As they walked, the linking of their hands seemed to grow…more important?

Not something to be tugged back from.

Maybe it was the cocktails. Maybe it was the night. Maybe it was the knowledge of each other, a realisation of vulnerability, of pain.

Or something deeper?

They reached their bungalow and it was time

for her to pull away, but as they paused on the veranda there seemed no impetus to go inside. The moonlight glimmered across the ocean, a bush turkey was shuffling in the undergrowth, but the feel of Ben's hand holding hers was suddenly...everything. The warmth, the strength, the solidness of his body.

His vulnerability? Why did that feel so important?

She was standing too close to him. She was feeling...

As she had no right to be feeling.

It was less than two months since she'd walked away from Mathew, less than two months since her mother had died. Ben had just talked to her of his dead wife. There was surely no room in this moment for these sensations.

But the sensations were present.

Ben's eyes were smiling but his smile looked uncertain. Was he feeling...what she was feeling?

They were two sensible, mature people, she told herself a little bit desperately. They had every reason to back away.

Except those good, sensible reasons were suddenly like threads of gossamer, fragile, impossible to grasp even if she wanted.

What was it about this night? This woman?

Maybe it wasn't Anya, Ben thought. Maybe

tonight had just been the culmination of things that had been building for ever.

Tonight was the first time he'd ever spoken honestly about his marriage. It was the first time he'd ever let someone glimpse the emptiness, the sadness, the betrayal, and the way he felt now was almost indescribable.

He'd never wanted to talk about his marriage. His time with Rihanna was his personal grief, his load to carry, but for some reason telling Anya seemed to have lifted something he'd hardly acknowledged was there.

Maybe it was this place, he thought, or was it what had happened today? This night out of time, this tropical paradise, the tensions and medical urgency of the afternoon, the unreal situation with Ricardo...they'd somehow jerked him out of his grey past.

Or was it being with Anya?

Whatever, the sensations he was feeling now were suddenly almost overwhelming. Heaviness had lifted, to be replaced by a lightness that made him feel almost dizzy. He was flooded with a vast feeling of freedom, of moving on. Of...the future? Anything was possible, he thought, feeling dazed. His time of bleakness was done.

And now... He was standing in the moonlight with a woman who was as beautiful as she was skilled, as kind as she was smart.

As desirable as...

As Anya.

He didn't have to move on. Anya was right here.

Anya was watching Ben's face, wondering what he was thinking. Watching the flood of emotions. Half-expecting him to back away, say goodnight, move on.

But then his uncertainty seemed to fade and his smile changed. Tenderness. Wonder. Need?

'Anya…' When he said her name there was a hoarseness in his voice, a depth that made something in her stomach clench. Something that made every thread of sense cut loose from its moorings and drift away.

'Anya,' he said again, and her other hand was held. And then he said it for the third time.

'Anya?'

And, with that, qualms, sense, the past, everything seemed to dissolve and there was no choice what to say.

'Yes,' she said, because a question had been asked and it had been answered.

The warmth of the night in this tropical paradise, the drama of the past day, weariness… or plain old-fashioned lust…were they reason enough for what she was feeling? Maybe she no longer needed a reason. What did matter was that his mouth was on hers and she was being kissed. Ruthlessly, deeply, magically, she was being kissed—or maybe *he* was being kissed.

Who'd instigated it? She didn't have a clue. Maybe she'd raised her mouth to his. She must have. If she had, it was entirely instinctive. She shouldn't want to make love with this man—surely she didn't?

But her body had different ideas. For whatever reason, she was standing at the entrance to a bungalow where the single bedroom had been divided in two—and every fibre of her being was flooded with the knowledge that there'd be no divider tonight.

Her mouth was under his, his tongue was tasting her, savouring, and she was taking the same sensations from him. Heat, want, pure animal desire.

All day as she'd worked with this man, this feeling had been building. She wanted him so much, but it was more than that. His confessions about his past marriage had made no difference—or maybe they'd added to what she was feeling. It was as if in this moment he was somehow...almost a part of her. And joining in any way they could seemed inevitable.

Her arms were around him, feeling the strength of him. Her hands slid under his shirt, feeling the breadth of his shoulders. Feeling the heat...

Oh, she wanted him.

His hands were under her blouse and the feeling was exquisite. She felt her breasts firm. She was crushed against him. His lovely long fingers were slipping into her bra and the feeling was… as if this was where she was meant to be.

Like two halves of a whole. Like a perfect solution.

It was no solution. She was surely sensible enough, aware enough, to know that this was—well, not sensible at all. But they were two mature adults, well past thinking a moment's passion meant a lifetime commitment. So surely…surely…

Oh, but she couldn't think. His hands… The feel of his body. The way her breasts were crushed against him, the way her feet seemed to arch upward so she could deepen the kiss…

And then he was pulling away, holding her at arm's length, but this was no finality. She could see desire in his eyes, a desire that matched hers.

And a touch of desperation that she understood.

'We can't,' she managed before he said it, but she knew—they both knew—that this break, this moment of intruding sense, was all about practicalities.

'We have a medical clinic next door.' His voice was unsteady, thick with desire. 'A ready-made pharmacy. Surely it'll stock…'

Of course it would. Her body almost seemed to sag in relief.

Practicalities. She was using no protection— her engagement was over, why should she? Ben didn't seem like a guy who carried condoms in his wallet just in case.

And neither of them was stupid.

Or maybe they were, just not stupid enough to have sex without any protection at all. But a ready stocked pharmacy…

'Wait here,' Ben growled, but she shook her head.

'You don't know where to look. Two of us can search much faster than one.'

'Anya…' She heard laughter in his voice, but she also heard something else she hadn't heard before. Happiness. Lightness. As if he was suddenly letting go of shadows.

As was she, she thought as Ben searched the information book for the access code to the clinic and they both headed through the adjoining door. So fast they almost blocked each other—the doorway was too narrow!

For heaven's sake, they were like two horny teenagers, in lust, aching for each other's bodies. But that was what she felt like—a kid again. This night was out of time. A crazy night where they were both in another world.

A world where, thankfully, they found a beautifully ordered clinic with everything clearly labelled. And in the bottom drawer of a medical supplies chest they found what they were looking for.

Ben held them up in triumph and they whooped like idiotic kids. And kissed.

And melted.

It was a miracle they didn't end up naked on the clinic floor. Somehow they ended up back in one of the beds.

Somehow they ended up exactly where they wanted to be.

Somehow they ended up together.

She woke and reality hit her like a sledgehammer.

What had she done? Was she nuts?

She wasn't nuts. She was exquisitely, wonderfully sated and if her fairy godmother was hovering to grant a wish, she'd wish she could spend the rest of her life in this man's arms.

Protected. Loved. Cherished.

But, almost as she woke, the first tentacles of doubt crept in as another word slammed into her head.

Grateful. Was she grateful for last night?

She was—she felt incredibly, deliriously grateful, but for some dumb reason the word was suddenly front and centre and it felt like a clang of warning. Maybe it *was* dumb, but it was there all the same. She'd had almost two months of independence, two months of not being grateful, two months of being…her.

She lay in the almost magical warmth of Ben's arms and she thought of letting this moment continue. She could continue this 'mock marriage'. They could take away the wardrobes, push the beds together and fall into the future.

But I don't even know who Anya is yet, she thought, suddenly panicked. I'm me, and I need to find out about me. Make love to this guy? Yes, because it was fabulous, it was the best feeling. It *is* the best feeling.

Except now she couldn't get up and head home to her place, to her independence, to a place where any decision about her future was taken by *her*.

It was too soon. Too fast.

And Ben… She thought of what he'd told her the night before. His marriage. His tragedy. Where did that leave him?

She'd hardly got her own life together. How could she help him?

Her heart seemed to be racing, and the medically trained side of her thought suddenly, Am I heading for more panic? She forced herself to breathe slowly, deeply. She closed her eyes, but all she could feel was the warmth of him, the strength. The need…

She wasn't panicking, she thought. These thoughts were realistic. They'd had an amazing night. Emotions had blasted away any semblance of sense, and now it was time for reality to reassert itself.

But not yet. His arms were still holding her. She could give herself these last few minutes, she thought. She could lie here and think…what if?

There was no future in *what if?*

Except…colleagues had become lovers before. If they gave themselves time…space.

Space? Somehow she had to regain it.

Somehow she would, but not quite yet. She'd take a couple more moments of feeling as if she was in the best place in the world.

A couple more moments of imagining life could be perfect.

He had Anya in his arms. She was spooned against his chest, gloriously naked, her skin warm against his. Her body was beautiful.

She was the most beautiful woman he'd ever met. This was where he wanted to be for the rest of his life.

Which was a crazy thing to think, and as he thought it his arms must have tightened. For she murmured and stirred and he felt her body shift a little.

His arms had been holding her, but he let her go. She twisted in the bed, his gaze met hers and he saw the expression in her eyes.

Dismay?

Sadness!

It was so far from what he was feeling that his gut lurched. He raised a hand to touch her face but she flinched.

'No.'

'No?'

'I've… I've been thinking. We can't. Ben, that was stupid.'

'It didn't feel stupid.'

That brought a glimmer of a smile into her eyes, but it was squashed fast.

'They already think we're married,' she said, and he could hear traces of panic.

'So we push the beds together.' He made his voice deliberately prosaic.

'And put rings on our fingers and get on with it?'

That made him pause. Like the lack of a condom the night before, sense raised its ugly head.

Once upon a time he'd fallen into lust and ended up married. No. This was way too soon. Too fast. Had he learned no lessons from the past?

And he saw the same flinch reflected in her eyes.

'No,' she said, softly now. 'Ben, this isn't going to work. I've been beholden all my life, and marriage for me… Well, it was just something that everyone expected. The inevitable. What's happened with us is different, but there's the same risk that we're falling for what's expected. We work together, we push the beds together, we...'

'Enjoy each other's bodies?'

'We both know we can't do that without... without an emotional connection.'

She was so beautiful. Her body was still touching his. She'd pulled away, but this bed was too narrow—and every part of him that touched her was screaming for more.

But the look in her eyes... It was almost desperation.

And he got it. Of course he got it. This was an impossible situation—to want her, for her to be so close and yet...

For sense to prevail. He needed to be sensible as well.

'I'll talk to Martin,' she was saying, softly but implacably. 'If there's no other accommodation and it's impossible for us to work here except as a practically married couple, then I'll resign.'

'No!'

'I suspect I won't need to. We saw yesterday how much they need two doctors, and we haven't broken our contract. Accommodation is provided in our contract and there was nothing there that said that meant a shared bedroom. They've made assumptions...'

'We let them make them.'

'You let them make them, and that assumption has to stop.' She took a deep breath and then slipped out of bed, and the wrench he felt was like physical pain. 'Ben, we know we need to be sensible.'

She tugged the top quilt from the bed and draped it around herself, cutting herself off from him even further. 'Ben, I need space. Martin must have a spare room somewhere on this island.'

She was talking sense—he knew she was. He thought of Rihanna all those years ago, smiling at him like the cat that had got the cream. *Darling, I'm pregnant. Surely it doesn't matter, though. It must means we'll have to get married faster.'*

Of all the stupid things to be thinking now... except he was thinking it.

'I'll find a room,' he told her, accepting the inevitable. 'You stay here.'

'Nope.' And here came that smile again, a trifle rueful but gorgeous all the same. 'Ben, I don't trust myself. There's no way I'm sleeping in a room that's one door away from a whole drawer full of condoms.'

'And me?'

'You can do what you like with them,' she said, and there was a wobble in her voice, but also defiant certainty. 'Ben, we're free and we need to stay that way.'

* * *

And that was that. She disappeared to her side of the wardrobes, to her ensuite bathroom, to her independence.

He headed for the other shower, he stood under steaming water and forced himself to think.

She was right. He knew she was. This had happened too fast. Yesterday had been fraught, but for Anya the last two months had been a roller coaster.

And for him?

Yesterday he'd been a doctor again. A true medic, performing at the top of his game.

He'd hardly practised medicine since the accident. The locum post at Merriwood had been planned to ease him back into his career, and this island job had been meant to be more of the same. An island retreat with a little easy medicine on the side. A way to slowly regain his medical confidence and give his body more time to recover.

But yesterday had demanded all his medical skills, and there'd been the same demand on his recovering body. What he'd managed…it had felt deeply satisfying.

And maybe what had happened last night had been more of the same. The old Ben resurfacing. A man in charge of his world. A man with a gorgeous woman.

But that woman needed even more time to recover than he did.

She was right. Falling into what the island would see almost as a formal relationship was impossible. Neither of them wanted it.

Really?

Cut it out, he told himself as his body stirred again. Get dressed, go see Martin, organise separate living arrangements.

Right.

Moving on.

Anya saw a tearful Mia in the clinic at nine, and by nine-thirty they had plans in place for her to leave the island.

'He's been hitting me for ever,' Mia admitted. 'But he's so gorgeous and so rich, and people think I'm so lucky.'

'Do you think you're lucky?' Anya asked gently, and got sobs in reply.

'I guess not,' she admitted at last. 'Not any more.'

'Then it's time to leave,' Anya told her. And then, looking at the woman in front of her, she softened. 'Hey, you'll be known as Ricardo's ex, a woman who walked away from him rather than the other way around. How much social cachet will that give you?'

'I guess,' she sniffed. 'But I'm scared.'

'Scared of leaving?'

'He'll be so angry.'

'We'll have Security with you until you leave the island,' Anya told her. 'Starting now. And believe me, it's so much better to walk away. There are so many other lovely guys out there— it's time you found a kind one.'

'Kind as well as gorgeous?' Mia said, her chin firming a little. 'Do they exist?'

'Yes, they do,' Anya told her—and tried very hard not to think of the guy she'd just spent the night with.

Enough. It was time to put that aside and figure how to move forward.

She organised one of the female security officers to meet them and help Mia pack, and then she went to find Ben. Then they walked silently across to the administration buildings to meet Martin.

But as she walked she kept thinking of Mia, silently packing and leaving.

It's for the best for me too, she told herself. But there's no comparison. I'm not exactly leaving the island—and Ben... Well, Mathew was kind too.

Mathew's kindness had felt very, very different.

Why?

She didn't understand, but she didn't have to. Get over it, she told herself. Just…make yourself separate.

They found Martin still reeling from the events of the day before, and he seemed almost confused at this new complication. In the face of the delay to the movie, with the associated mass cancellation, this must have seemed almost trivial. He listened, seemingly almost bemused, as Ben apologised for the misunderstanding, blaming himself.

Then Anya told him they'd wondered if splitting the bedroom would work but one night had convinced her it wouldn't.

'He snores,' Anya said blandly, and Martin looked at them for a long moment and maybe came to his own conclusions.

But the bottom line was that the jet-ski incident had shaken him badly, he was in damage control mode and this was a minor hiccup he needed to deal with fast.

At another time he might have objected, knowing that allocating more accommodation would hurt his bottom line. But without these two doctors he might well have been explaining deaths to the circling media, rather than admittedly horrific injuries.

'The island's two doctors were on the scene within minutes...' It had sounded okay in the piece the island's publicity officer had released. If one of those doctors walked away this morning it would look bad.

The delay in filming meant that the resort

was no longer fully booked. There was a studio apartment empty, and thus Anya could move straight in.

Sorted. They came out and stood in the sunshine and Ben smiled ruefully down at her.

'Done. Now for that "walk in the park" future we promised ourselves. I'm heading for a swim. What about you?'

'Not with you,' she said, and then tempered it. 'Sorry. That sounded…ungrateful.'

'But I never wanted you to be grateful,' he told her. 'In fact, it's the last thing I want. So separate everything?'

'Apart from medicine.'

'And the odd piña colada on the terrace at night?'

'Not me,' she replied, and managed a smile to match his. 'After last night…piña coladas seem very dangerous indeed.'

CHAPTER NINE

No!

What had followed was six weeks of letting her world settle. It had also been six weeks of working side by side with Ben. That had involved initial strain, but their jobs had continued to be more demanding than they'd expected. They'd needed to work both separately and in partnership and, as they had, the sexual tension between them had finally faded.

But it hadn't disappeared, Anya conceded, and when she woke six weeks after their arrival she decided it must be tension that was making her so exhausted.

It couldn't be anything else. Her little studio was perfect. The workload might be greater than they'd expected but it wasn't huge. She'd had time to swim, to snooze in the sun, to get to know the resort staff. To think that this job was actually pretty awesome.

But for some reason she couldn't relax when Ben was around. Every time he was near, her body seemed to tingle. To demand that she be closer.

She'd worked late with him the night before, treating an asthmatic guest whose husband had been so terrified Ben had called for her to back him up.

He'd walked her back to her studio in the moonlight, and there were those nerve-endings again, all pointing in the one direction, screaming at her to...

To do nothing, she'd told herself harshly, but it had taken her ages to go to sleep. She still felt tired and when she'd made herself toast she'd thought, Do I really want to eat it?

And then, as she stared at her uneaten toast, she'd thought... *No!*

Appalled, she'd slipped across to the clinic, found what she needed—and now she was staring at a double blue line.

No, no and no!

And then, as her world seemed to turn into a dizzy maelstrom of emotion, Joe arrived—holding a turtle. A small one, its shell not much bigger than a dinner plate, its shell cracked, its neck extended and oozing blood.

'Reckon it's been hit by one of the buggies,' Joe said while she stood at the door and tried to make her mind focus. 'I found it on the track coming up from the beach. Ben's out having his morning swim so I brought him to you. You reckon there's anything you can do?'

Okay. Somehow she pulled herself together, back into medical mode. Everything else—or just one thing else—had to be put on the back-burner.

She and Ben spilt their workload as much as they could so they could work separately, but she looked at the little turtle and knew it needed them both.

This was another aspect of her job she hadn't counted on. It seemed Medical Officer meant coping with injured wildlife as well, and where was that in the small print of their contract? It wasn't there, but there was no way the resort would pay for helicopter transfer for a damaged turtle.

'In the past we've put them down,' Joe had said the first time he'd presented them with a sad, dehydrated possum. 'The last docs wouldn't have anything to do with anything that wasn't human, but I'm hoping you're different. If you can fix this guy so he can survive till the next ferry run, I can organise a wildlife carer on the mainland to take over. There's a vet on the main-land, Rob Lewis, who'll talk you through any-thing you need to know. He's sent me a great handbook but it's too complicated for me to fol-low anything more than "Keep 'em quiet, keep 'em warm". So what about it, docs? Can we occasionally give you a different kind of patient?'

And that was what this turtle was. A *very* different kind of patient.

She looked down at the broken shell and the lacerated neck, and her distracted mind settled in the face of medical need. A vet was surely the way to go, but the next ferry to the mainland wasn't scheduled until Friday, and the little creature's odds of surviving until then were minimal.

'Let's get him to the clinic. I'll get him warm while you let Ben know what's happening,' she told Joe.

Her shock, her emotions needed to be put aside, but…now she'd be operating with Ben. Did she need to tell him?

The thought made her dizzy.

Whatever.

Shock was still making her numb, but she had work to do, she told herself as she carried the little turtle across to the clinic. She needed to phone their friendly vet and get some advice, and then set up their mini theatre.

In the last weeks Martin had agreed to them buying equipment to cope with such situations— it was a good look for the island, he'd conceded, to have a wildlife first aid station he could brag about. One of their first patients had been a go-anna with an injured leg and that had meant heating was required.

Reptiles, including goannas and turtles, were cold-blooded. That meant their blood was the same temperature as the atmosphere, and if they were cold everything slowed. Normally that was okay, but anaesthetics depended on a reasonable blood flow to make them effective. So while she made her call to the mainland vet, writing down everything she needed to know about surgery on turtles—or all the information she could get in one phone call—she was also pushing up the clinic's heating, and then pumping up the hot pad.

By the time Ben arrived she had the place cosy warm—or a bit too warm. Okay for a turtle, but for her...

'Are you okay?' Ben asked. He'd walked in the door and stopped and looked at her.

She shrugged. 'I think so.' She managed a smile. 'I usually wear make-up, but Joe handing me a turtle when I was still mid-breakfast put paid to that.' No need to tell him that her breakfast hadn't been touched.

He smiled back, but gave her a long look. 'You're up to this?'

'Hey, it's not brain surgery. I've designated you as surgeon. I'm on breathing. Our instructions are here. Right to go?'

Another searching look. Disconcerting.

He was disconcerting. He'd also obviously dressed in a hurry—Joe must have met him at the beach. Island gear. Shorts, sandals, an open-necked shirt, tousled damp hair.

Six weeks on the island had seen his already tanned skin turn a deep golden. The swimming had also improved the strength of his leg. He often abandoned his cane, and his limp was becoming less pronounced.

He looked…

No! Don't go there!

He was flicking through the sheets she'd written. Most of the instructions were on how to intubate a turtle, which would be her job. Then he was checking the little turtle, examining the cracked shell.

'If we took that piece off…' he said, considering. 'It's not huge and, according to your notes, it should regrow. It'll spoil his beauty, though.'

'We'll tell him to stop looking in mirrors,' she managed, cutting off thoughts that were spinning in every direction other than where they needed to go. 'Ready when you are.'

'Right,' he said, but he cast her another long look. 'Let's go.'

Intubating a turtle was like intubating a newborn. Tricky. It should feel far less stressful, she thought, as she set up the hose and taped the airway into position, but the turtle's head was tiny, maybe less than ten centimetres wide. So maybe it was even harder than intubating a newborn. But the vet manual had pictures, the instructions had been clear, and luckily her fingers stayed steady enough to cope.

And once she had everything in place, once the anaesthetic took effect—heavens, they'd had to make the place warm!—it was a matter of monitoring and watching Ben work.

He was good. Really good.

The tiny head had a deep laceration along the side and the rough, leathery skin was grazed and filthy. 'Someone driving too fast,' Joe had growled. 'Our buggies are only supposed to go at ten kilometres an hour but they'll push faster downhill, and that's where we found this little guy. I like to think the idiot who hit him didn't realise, otherwise I'd be pushing Martin to kick him off the island.'

Me too, Anya thought, but her concentration was almost solely on Ben.

He was gently, carefully probing the wound, removing tiny bits of gravel, making sure the lesion was completely clean before he closed. That was easier said than done when the gravel was the same colour as the turtle. But he had all the patience in the world, and with the wound cleaned he stitched it closed and then looked at the shell.

'I reckon we can do this too,' he said. 'It could

wait for a vet, but it'd mean another anaesthetic. You up for another twenty minutes or so?'

Why was he asking? Did she look that wobbly?

'Cut it out,' she growled. 'I'll stop wearing make-up entirely if losing it has this effect on my colleagues.'

That resulted in another searching look, but he nodded then turned his attention back to the shell.

A piece almost as big as a small egg had cracked, and Ben had folded it away while he tended to the neck wound.

'Rob assured me it'll regrow,' she told Ben. 'Not as smoothly, but eventually. He'll need to stay in a wildlife refuge until it does.'

'Well, he'll be a quiet little guest and I'm guessing he won't eat much.' He looked again at the shell. 'This isn't a clean break—see how the edges are shattered and the piece itself is broken? We'll keep what we can in case the wildlife vets want to wire and cement it together, but if we leave it like it is those edges are likely to pierce his skin. I can cut away the piece that'll lie over the wound itself, and the damage isn't so big that it'll leave him exposed where it matters.'

She nodded and went back to checking the airway, then figuring what was needed to keep the little creature anaesthetised for longer. And trying not to think about the searching look Ben had just given her.

And trying not to think…how to tell him. The prospect was pretty close to blindsiding her.

It was just as well she needed to focus on the job at hand, she decided, otherwise she might well have fainted, and it wasn't just the heat that was doing it to her. She stayed fiercely concentrating as Ben carefully removed the broken part of the shell, debrided the edges, swabbed, dressed and finally said, 'Right, we're done. He might even live because of us.'

He stood back from the table and watched as she checked and rechecked, then removed the intubation gear, as she cleared her stuff away, as she carried the heated pad into a little enclosure they'd set up in the storeroom for the wildlife they'd already treated, as she finally had no excuse but to stop being busy.

'Anya,' he said as she came back into the clinic, and she met his gaze and she knew exactly what was coming.

'I… Yes?'

'Is there any chance you could be pregnant?'

Pregnant. The word seemed to explode in her head. *Pregnant!*

How had he guessed?

'Anya?' He was on the far side of the operating table. He was watching her with concern, but also…what else?

Horror?

That was too strong a word, she thought. It was too strong a word for what she was feeling, too.

Or was it?

There was a seat by the desk. She pulled it out and sat down, hard. There was no way she could avoid this. No way she couldn't tell the truth.

'I just did a test,' she whispered. 'I…yes.'

There was a moment's appalled silence.

She was forcing her fuzzy mind to think… the unthinkable. It was six weeks since they'd had sex. Six weeks! And two months before that since her abandoned wedding.

Her cycle…

'I had an IUD.' She was stammering. 'After the wedding… I removed it, there was no use for it, but it's taken a while for things to settle. It often does.'

'So you haven't had a period?'

'You're not my doctor,' she flashed, suddenly angry. Surely this wasn't a conversation she should be having with him.

It was a conversation she should be having with herself.

She was already having it.

'We used a condom.' She said it out loud, almost defiantly. 'We're not stupid.'

He didn't answer. Instead, with an expression on his face she couldn't read, he rounded the table and pulled open one of the drawers that held pharmaceutical supplies.

Right down the bottom was a box containing what they'd found that night. Condoms, all in their original wrappers.

'I didn't think.' His tone was blank, hollow. 'It was our first night here. I didn't check…'

'You didn't check what?'

'You know that they sell these in the resort gift shop,' he said, still in that empty voice. 'I've seen them there. They sell basic things like paracetamol, sticking plasters, antiseptic. Maybe when the resort first opened they put everything here, but the doctors would have fast become tired of being woken to supply such things. How long's the gift shop been open? If these have been sitting here since then…'

He held one up, he read the label—and then he blenched.

'Wh…what?' she stammered.

There was a long, loaded silence. And then, in a voice she hardly recognised, he said, 'Anya, their expiry date is over ten years ago.'

Her thoughts suddenly veered, strangely, to her mother. Telling her of how she'd come to live in Australia.

Anya, I was pregnant. I didn't have a choice but to follow your father.

Choice.

Her mother had wanted to be a teacher. She'd just won a scholarship to one of the Philippines' top universities.

But then she'd met Anya's father, a visiting tourist, and that had been that. Pregnancy, marriage, leaving everything she knew to travel to a life of isolation—and the endless need for gratitude.

Maybe even the fact that her father had offered to marry her had been cause for gratitude.

But this was different, Anya told herself frantically. Far, far different.

So why was she instinctively touching her belly and thinking…of tuna bakes?

There were so many emotions, he couldn't get them in any sort of order.

He was looking at Anya's face, seeing her instinctive move to touch her belly, realising she was as shocked as he was. Looking at her hand on her belly, he accepted it as absolute truth.

But he'd been down this road before. *'Ben, I'm pregnant.'*

The shock.

Years seemed to fall away. Once again he was that nerdy kid, staring in horror as Rihanna made her announcement. He was back seeing the sophisticated woman he thought he knew, sobbing in what he'd realised afterwards was well acted terror and knowing without doubt there was only one road to follow.

And now… His world seemed to fade into some sort of mindless fog and, before he even realised he was about to say it, the words were out of his mouth.

'I… We'll have to get married.'

Why…*why* had he said that? It was crazy, stupidly inappropriate, completely out of kilter with everything that should be said. It was a gut reaction, a repeat of what had gone before, and he knew how wrong it was the moment the words were out of his mouth. And Anya's face reflected it. She stared up at him and flinched as if she'd been struck, and then she stood and faced him with horror.

'Don't you dare,' she managed.

'Dare?'

'No! What are you saying? Marriage? Are you out of your mind? What the…? Am I supposed to fall at your feet in gratitude for such an offer? This isn't the last century, Ben. This is my body, my life.'

'But I…'

'You what? Impregnated me? So you're the noble guy who'll do his duty? Because of what? Guilt? Go jump.'

'Anya…'

'No.' She caught herself and her hands flew

to her cheeks, as if she was trying to somehow keep her head steady on her shoulders. 'This is crazy, but I need to think.'

'We do. Anya, this is our decision.'

He was trying to say it was a shared responsibility, that he wouldn't walk away, that this wasn't all on her shoulders, but she read it wrong. Okay, he'd said it wrong.

'I think we both know that's not true,' she said, and she closed her eyes. And when she opened them her face was set.

'Look after the turtle,' she managed. 'I only… I only realised myself this morning. You're on call and I need time to get my head in order. Ben, I need to be by myself.'

And without another word she walked out.

He felt as if he'd been punched. No, this sensation was bigger than any punch could be. It was overwhelming.

The memory of Rihanna was all around him, her two declarations of pregnancy, the way he'd felt.

This was different. It had to be.

But still, the feeling of entrapment was inescapable. One stupid mistake, a night of overblown emotion, and now consequences.

He remembered his student self, looking at the gorgeous Rihanna in horror as she'd announced her pregnancy. Those emotions had surged to the fore as he'd realised Anya was pregnant.

They were wrong.

Still, though, they'd been inescapable—they were almost a muscle memory.

This *was* different, though, he told himself. Anya didn't want him. She didn't expect anything. It was only his honour…

Was it?

The memory of Anya's face was still with him, blanched with shock. He'd wanted to hold her, to comfort her, to say…

We'll have to get married?

Stupid, stupid, stupid.

But what had been the alternative? Go down on one knee and propose? Pretend marriage had been in his mind before?

She was right, he thought as he checked the heating pad under the little turtle and watched it resurface to a bewildering new reality.

That was what he was facing, he thought. A new reality.

It was just as bewildering.

Anya was right, he decided. They both needed time to get their heads in order. They needed to be…by themselves?

Maybe they did. He was in unchartered territory and the kaleidoscope of conflicting emotions was refusing to settle.

Nothing had to be settled today, he told himself. Life could go on as normal.

Anya was pregnant.

They were pregnant.

Suddenly there seemed no such thing as normal.

CHAPTER TEN

THEY MANAGED TO stay apart for nearly three days.

As long as there were no crises that was possible, even on an island the size of Dolphin. They alternated clinic duty, and they also alternated call-outs to the individual villas. Over the last six weeks they'd often gone together, but now, unless it was imperative, they worked alone.

Because they needed to get their heads around…

Pregnancy. The future. Ties that neither of them wanted.

Or did they?

Realisation of the pregnancy had seemed to hit Anya like a blow to the side of her head. One part of her was busy castigating herself for being unbelievably stupid. Another was railing at Ben for his insensitivity, his crass proposal.

The biggest part of her was responding with panic.

But three days was a long time in the life of a woman who'd just learned she was pregnant, and by the end of the third day she'd reached a few conclusions. Which, she decided on that third afternoon, was only fair she share.

She knew Ben had received a call to the marine research centre—someone with chest pain. She'd heard the call come in on the receivers they both carried. She'd offered to go with him—their need for solitude didn't extend to medical emergencies—but Ben had knocked her back.

'The manager's pretty sure it's a panic attack—the guy's had them before and he has a research paper that's overdue. I'll contact you if I need you.'

So she knew where he was, and she knew he'd be coming home. To *his* home next to the clinic. Her home was two pathways away. Her studio apartment was small enough for most tourists to turn their noses up, but it was perfect for her. As she closed the door behind her and headed towards Ben's she thought, I want to stay here.

Which was pretty much what she wanted to say to Ben.

When Ben returned Anya was sitting on the front steps of his bungalow. The sun was sinking behind the island. Lorikeets were coming in to roost, and their raucous calls filled the night. The island was settling to sleep.

The setting was lovely. And the woman on the step was lovely. Dressed in shorts and an oversized shirt tied at the waist, her hair tumbling to her shoulders, she looked relaxed and calm, a million miles from the woman he'd met only a few months before.

But as he got nearer he saw the look of tension in her eyes. She was here to say something important—he knew it—and he felt his own tension surge to match.

'Hey,' he said warily.

'Hey yourself. It was a panic attack, then?'

He nodded. 'Apparently his research paper— differential wave motion affecting specific coral spawning...' He smiled but it was an effort. He could almost taste the tension between them.

'I know, I can't wait to read it too,' he managed. 'But I gather it has to be submitted by tomorrow or it'll miss the publication schedule, which means missing out on funding. His pride hasn't let him ask for help, but once he admitted it we organised colleagues to help. They'll stay up until midnight or longer or until it's done.'

'So heart attack fixed?'

'I wish they were all that easy.' He reached the base of the steps and looked down at her. 'I'd offer you a drink but I see you already have one.'

'Iced water,' she told him, raising her glass. 'Isn't it lucky I swore off piña coladas on that first night and haven't had an alcoholic drink since? It's as if I knew.'

'I can't believe you didn't.'

Her face froze, and once again he thought, What am I, an idiot?

'I didn't know,' she said flatly.

'Anya, I'm sorry. That was a crass thing to say. Of course I believe you.'

'It doesn't matter.'

'It does matter,' he said and sat down beside her. 'Anya…'

'I'm going to keep it.'

He was silent, letting her statement settle, not game to open his mouth unless something else stupid came out. So it was Anya who spoke next.

'And I'd like to stay on this island,' she said, almost defiantly.

'Anya…' Why wasn't his brain engaging his mouth?

'This place is perfect.' She was speaking in a rush, as if she had to get the words out fast. 'It's early days but if…if my pregnancy stays… viable…my little studio will be big enough for me and a baby, at least for a couple of years. I can use the island creche. I'll need to take a few weeks off after the birth, but if you're still here you can cover for me. If not… If you decide to leave… Hannah—you've met Martin's wife?—she told me scores of doctors applied for the position. It'll be easy enough to get someone else. They *did* want a couple, but they like us, they've accepted our arrangement, so nothing will change.'

Nothing will change? He thought…baby? Everything would change.

But all he said was, 'You talked to Hannah?'

'I had to talk to someone,' she told him. 'Their kids are older now, of course, but she said this is an idyllic spot to raise them. You know there's a little school here for the kids of the resort and the research station, and as they get older the resort subsidises boarding school fees on the mainland. Apparently, they need that to attract permanent staff. And Hannah will support me.'

I had to talk to someone. Hannah will support me.

Why was his stomach clenching at those words?

He remembered the overwhelming feeling of being trapped when Rihanna had announced her pregnancy. That feeling had flooded back three days ago but now Anya's calm words had dispelled it completely.

He missed it? Did he want to be trapped?

This wasn't a trap. This was just…what happened when people were stupid. It was what happened when people were in lust.

Or in love.

Love. Where had that word come from?

'So where do I fit in all this?' he asked slowly.

'I guess…wherever you want to fit—short of marriage,' she added hastily. 'I thought, initially, not at all. The last thing I want is commitment because you feel obligated. But if you'd like to be a part-time dad…if you stay on the island… maybe we could work things out. Or even if you don't stay…other people have worked co-parenting. But only if you want it, Ben. This baby might like a father, but not one who's doing it from guilt—or for me. I don't need it. Be very clear, I don't need you.'

It was like a slap.

It was so different from Rihanna's announcement of pregnancy that he was having trouble taking it in.

But suddenly he knew what he wanted to say. What he had to say.

'I'd like to share.'

This time his words went down better. The tension in her eyes seemed to soften. There was a long silence and then she nodded.

'Sharing might be good,' she said softly. 'But Ben, it's early days yet. We both know nothing's settled. Even if it does… I mean…' Her hands automatically seemed to move to her tummy. Protectively? 'There's plenty of time to organise access, formal agreements.'

'Would we want formal agreements?'

'I don't know.' She gave another decisive nod, as if she'd covered everything she needed to cover, and stood up. 'We'll figure it out, but that's all I wanted to say tonight. I'll leave you to come to terms with it.'

'You don't want to have dinner with me?'

She stared down at him, and her face closed again. 'In preparation for you to tell me again we need to get married?'

'That was stupid.'

'Yes, it was,' she said, briskly now. 'This baby's nothing to do with…well, with obligation. Let's figure things out formally. There's no other way.'

CHAPTER ELEVEN

IT SEEMED SHE had a village.

Where had this come from? During her first weeks on the island almost all her attention had been on the resort and its guests, but behind the scenes was a working community. The research centre had permanent staff, many with families, and most of the resort staff were permanent as well.

When Anya had first learned she was pregnant she'd hardly known them, but that one conversation with Martin's wife had been taken by Hannah as a need for support. Hannah had asked if Anya wanted the news kept secret. Anya had wondered whether there was any point. The news had thus spread, and almost within minutes the other mums on the island had collectively gathered her into their 'tribe'.

She was astute enough to realise, though, that their friendship, their support, their offers of help, weren't made out of charity. She was now their local doctor, the one they called when little Ollie had earache, or little Joey broke his toe. She wasn't an outsider who needed help, she was accepted as one of them.

She was thankful but she didn't need to thank. The sensation was great.

Strangely, though, it was Ben who now seemed the outsider. Because she wouldn't let him in? Or because he didn't want to be…in.

She hadn't told Hannah it was Ben who was the father. She hadn't told anyone. She'd also been deliberately vague about dates, and the islanders had decided on an alternative all by themselves. Apparently, someone knew someone who lived at Merriwood. Rumours of her disastrous wedding had thus spread, and her pregnancy was assumed to be part of the same disaster.

Regardless, the locals seemed to have collectively decided to respect her privacy, and she figured if Ben wanted to announce impending fatherhood it was up to him.

Which left them in a strange type of limbo.

She'd half-expected him to plan on leaving the island. This was a great place for him—his leg was strengthening almost daily—but surely he could soon go back to his career as an emergency medicine specialist.

But he gave no indication of leaving.

They therefore worked together. As the weeks

went by they relaxed enough to figure a way to get by, but the future was uncharted and undiscussed.

He seemed to think talking about her pregnancy was off-limits, and maybe it was.

How much did he want to be involved?

How much did she want him to be involved?

As the weeks rolled on, she came to terms with the stupidity of his crazy proposal. She accepted that it had been about Rihanna, a reaction to his appalling marriage. They both needed time to come to terms with this new normal.

She didn't need him, though, she continued to tell herself. She had her life on track and one moment's stupidity should surely not keep Ben from his own path.

At twelve weeks she took the ferry over to Cairns and had her first scan. That was a bit weird, a bit confronting, a bit…lonely? Maybe she should have asked Hannah to go with her. Or Ben? He'd offered, but the thought had made something inside her cringe. Wanting that of him…it'd be demanding responsibility and she wouldn't do it.

But as she looked at the scan, at the grainy image on the screen, for the first time she felt a pang of something that had nothing to do with either herself or Ben. This was a new little… person.

And with it came the realisation that this new little person had rights as well.

Like it or not, she had to let Ben closer.

'I brought you the ultrasound image. If…if you're interested.'

It was late afternoon. Ben had been sitting on the bungalow steps watching the light slowly turn golden over the sea. Anya approached looking…nervous.

He'd known where she'd been—of course he had—and he'd hated the thought that she was going alone. But she'd been adamant, as she'd been for weeks, answering every query about her pregnancy factually but with any offer of help being met with, 'Ben, I don't need you.'

'Is everything okay?' he asked now. He was watching her face as she came nearer. Dammit, he should have insisted on going.

He hated that she wouldn't let him.

'Everything's fine.'

'That's…great.' He could have been anyone, he thought. A friend. A colleague. Even a casual acquaintance asking if she was well.

If *their* baby was well.

He guessed most couples would be super excited right now, but he and Anya most definitely weren't *most couples*.

Anya was wearing her normal work gear, casual trousers and blouse. Her hair was tied tightly back and she look almost businesslike. Maybe that was deliberate, he thought. What was between them—should it be businesslike for ever?

This woman made him feel so conflicted.

The last few weeks had seen him flooded with emotions so confusing they were impossible to get his head around. One part of him wanted to be with her, support her, do…well, what he'd suggested the moment he'd learned of the pregnancy. Protect, cherish, take on full responsibility for the child she was carrying. But there was another part that maybe she understood better than he did.

She stepped forward but she didn't climb the steps to the veranda. Instead, she handed the print up to him.

He looked at the grainy black and white image and he didn't say a word.

So many emotions. What he was feeling…how could he even begin to understand? *His child.*

He looked to Anya and her face looked almost wooden.

'Ten fingers, ten toes, but tricky to tell the sex yet,' she said, her voice almost emotionless. 'We tried to figure it out but couldn't.'

'We?'

'The sonographer and I.'

And again that cut deep. It should have been him.

'Anya, I do want to be involved.'

'That's your right.'

'I mean…' How to say this? How to even mean something he didn't understand himself? 'With you,' he ventured. 'With us and our…our baby. Anya, what's between you and me…'

'There's nothing.' Was that a defence?

'It doesn't feel like nothing. Underneath all the baggage…'

'Yeah, the baggage,' she said, grimly now. 'There's way too much baggage. I would never, ever want you to think you were forced into another relationship—and I can see by your face that that's exactly what you're feeling.'

'I'm not.'

But was he? Honestly, he didn't have a clue. He and Rihanna had been together for so long that the feeling of obligation, of entrapment, was almost bone-deep. How to tell Anya that it wasn't obligation or guilt that made him want to take this relationship forward?

That made him want Anya for herself?

He couldn't, because he wasn't sure himself. And he met her gaze now and he could see that she knew it.

'Leave it, Ben,' she said, her voice gentling. 'You're an honourable man, and this baby will be lucky to have you as a dad. That's a pretty big step to take without…the rest. There's no need to force things.'

'I'd never force things.'

'I know you wouldn't.

'But I do want more involvement.' He stared down at the picture again and something inside him twisted. *His baby.* 'The next scan...' he said, trying to think forward. 'The normal scheduling's five months. Yes?'

'I...yes.'

'So in eight weeks, would you let me come?'

'I don't need...'

'I know you don't need, but maybe I need. Please, Anya.'

And her reply came fast, almost a gut reaction. 'Ben, I'm scared of letting you close.'

She said it too loud, too fast, and it was as if the words had been forced out. They hung between them, loaded.

'I guess the same might be said for me,' he said at last, and reluctantly he handed back the photograph. 'But we're doing a pretty good job of being independent now. Just, can you let me be involved? I accept you don't need me, but I can surely be involved with our baby without either of us needing each other.'

But was that even true? His thoughts were jumbling again. The way she looked, standing in the fading light, the honesty in her gaze, the tinge of fear...

What he wanted right now was to walk down the steps between them and gather her into his arms. To hold her against his body. To hold her against his heart?

Because she was vulnerable? Because he could see the fear in her eyes?

Because she was lovely?

It was all of those things, but strangely it was fear that held him back. But her fear or his? What she'd gone through... What they'd both gone through... He knew it was too soon, for Anya and for him.

So somehow he made himself hand back the photograph and smile.

'Thank you for showing me this. I'd like a copy.'

'To stick on your fridge?' She managed a rueful smile in return. I'll have it on *my* fridge, but if you put up a matching one the whole island will know.'

'I wouldn't mind.'

'But I would,' she said, hurriedly now. 'I know we'll eventually have to admit our...connection...but please Ben, not yet.'

'But the five-month scan...'

'Okay, I'd like you to come.' Her chin came up, semi-defiant. 'To be honest, it felt a bit lonely today. And I'll tell you...when...when I feel the first kick. Whenever I'm worried. I will keep you informed.'

'Informed doesn't mean involved.'

'I can't help that,' she managed. 'That's as far as I'm brave enough to go. Goodnight, Ben.'

The flash of fear on her face was unmistakable and, without another word, she turned and walked away. He was left on the step, looking after her.

He wanted…

No.

Emotional baggage was still there in spades, for both of them. He didn't know what he wanted.

Or maybe deep down he did, but he didn't have a clue how to get it.

Eight weeks later she was due to have her mid-pregnancy check-up and ultrasound. She made the appointment on the resort's changeover day. The ferry took guests to the mainland, then docked for a few hours, restocking supplies before bringing the next batch of guests back. That'd be plenty of time to have her check-up and do a little shopping—her clothes were now being stretched to the limit. Everything was sorted.

Except she had to tell Ben. With hardly any guests on the island it should be safe for both of them to leave, but they'd hardly talked about her pregnancy over the past eight weeks. Would he still want to come?

He'd been almost deliberately distant for the last few weeks. When he wasn't working, he'd been fiercely focusing on rebuilding his fitness.

They acted as colleagues only, providing a great medical service, working together as needed but at all other times being completely separate.

And Ben was more separate than she was. While she seemed to be fitting into island life, making friends, Ben was more and more a loner. She watched him swimming endless laps of the cove, driving himself to exhaustion. She saw him through the huge plate glass windows of the resort gym, pitting himself against the most challenging equipment. She saw him limping without his cane when surely it would have been easier to continue using it.

He seemed driven, and not just by the need to rebuild his strength.

Part of her ached to help, but there was nothing she could do. His demons were his own.

And as the date for her five-month scan approached part of her was still cringing about having him join her. Why? Because she was scared that he'd see it as a cry for help? As a need for his involvement?

Would that involvement mean more demons for Ben? Part of her knew that it would.

Those first words were still echoing in her mind, as they'd echoed now for months.

'We'll have to get married.'

She was sure that had been his demons speaking.

But she had demons of her own. She could still

hear her mother's words echoing down through the years.

'Your father and I had to get married. There was no choice.'

Well, times were different, she told herself, as she'd been telling herself for months. There was no way she was heading into forced matrimony.

But, like it or not, Ben *was* going to be her baby's father and she'd promised.

With the date confirmed, she asked him. They'd been doing a dressing together—one of the researchers had cut himself on coral and had a spreading ulcer that needed careful debridement. As they left the clinic she forced herself to sound nonchalant.

'By the way,' she managed. 'No pressure, but my scan's booked on Friday. So, if you're still interested, you're welcome to…to come with me.'

The last few words came out in a rush, and when she finished the silence seemed loaded.

But he simply nodded, like someone restructuring his diary in his head.

'I can make it.' The words were formal. Cautious?

'Only if you want…'

'Anya, I do want to meet our baby.'

Our baby.

Unconsciously her hands moved to her belly. Was that a whisper of movement? A tiny ripple?

Our baby.

'Martin says it's okay.' Again, she spoke too fast, repeating herself. 'It'll only be for a few hours...'

'You know I want to come.'

His voice was steady, sure. She glanced up at him and his eyes met hers. There was a message in those eyes. *I'm here for you.* And more. *I'm part of this.*

And with that came a stab of something akin to terror. Oh, for heaven's sake... Why was she so afraid of how this man made her feel?

Regardless, two days later she was lying on an examination table in the X-ray department of Cairns Central, her tummy covered with slippery gel, the wand of the ultrasound tracking back and forth over her skin.

And on the screen...

Her baby?

No. *Their* baby. Because when she glanced at Ben's face she saw her awe and wonder reflected back at her.

'It truly is,' he murmured, and she flinched at that.

'Did you think...'

'Oh, Anya, of course I didn't.' His hand covered hers and she was aware of a stab of... warmth? Something more?

Definitely more, but there were ghosts in the

way he held her hand, ghosts she didn't want to think about.

Maybe she had to.

'But Rihanna…' Why had she said that? Surely their mutual ghosts had nothing to do with here and now.

'This is nothing to do with Rihanna,' he said, but she heard a catch in his voice that told her there *was* a comparison being made. Those years of lies and manipulation had made their mark. 'Anya, we have a daughter.'

'A daughter?' she said, startled, and the sonographer chuckled.

'That's the problem with doctors' pregnancies. I don't get to spring surprises—boy, girl, twins.' She looked closely at the screen herself. 'Yep, it's a girl.'

'A daughter…' Anya hadn't looked—she simply didn't care—but now, looking closely…

Their little girl wasn't coyly holding her legs together. She was definitely…

Her daughter.

Their daughter?

She was thinking suddenly of her mum, a student, scared, alone, starring at an image on the screen of her, of Anya.

And then she was thinking of her father, Mike, staring at the screen as well.

Ben's words were exploding in her head. *We have a daughter.*

And suddenly she thought…no wonder her mother had travelled half a world from everything she knew and loved, to be with the father of her baby. Ben was still holding her hand and the link felt suddenly unbreakable.

We have a daughter…

Family?

She found she was crying, stupid, helpless tears that tracked down her face before she could stop them. And then Ben was wiping her tears and bending down so his face almost touched hers.

'Hey, it's okay. Please don't cry. It's great. It's wonderful.'

'I… I know. It's just…' She couldn't make herself go on. There seemed no words for what was in her heart.

And then Ben filled the silence for her.

'Anya, please, we need to be married.'

And then he too stopped.

The words hung in the air.

The sonographer was still at work, recording images, making sure measurements fitted with stage of pregnancy, checking, checking, checking to make sure everything was okay.

It *was* okay.

We need to be married.

Her overwhelming instinct right now was to melt into the warmth, the emotion, the…*love?*… that was in this room right now.

She couldn't. Because underneath the emotion were still the stupid, inexplicable seeds of fear.

Fear of what? She was no longer sure, but she knew she had to act on it.

'She looks perfect,' the sonographer said, briskly now. She'd obviously decided to ignore the undercurrents of emotion—or were they over-currents? They were so strong... Maybe sonographers were used to it. 'Your obstetrician will confirm, but I think you two can go out and celebrate that you have a gorgeous little girl in there and she's growing just as she should.' She grinned then. 'You know, a lot of parents take a babymoon at this stage.'

'A babymoon?' Anya asked stupidly. She was struggling to sit up. Ben tried to help but she pushed his hand away. Enough.

'Before your bump gets in the way.' Maybe the sonographer wasn't as astute as Anya had thought—or maybe she'd missed that push as Anya had rejected Ben's helping hand. 'Sort of like a honeymoon where you can enjoy being just you two.' She grimaced. 'You know, I have four kids and I love them to bits but from the time they were born they've been in my life every waking minute. If Warwick and I had our time again and had the chance of a babymoon, we'd be off like a shot. You two should go for it.'

'Maybe we will,' Ben said as he stood back to let Anya rise all by herself. 'I know a great resort. How about it, Anya? How about heading for Dolphin Isles Resort?'

It was an attempt to break the ice and it did—sort of. She gave him a weak smile and struggled to her feet.

'I'll meet you in the cafeteria after I'm dressed,' she managed, then thanked the beaming sonographer and grabbed her basket of clothes and headed for the changing rooms. But when she got there she sat hard on the bench and stared at nothing.

'Anya, please, we need to be married.'

Think, she told herself. Think!

'We need to be married.'

That was what her mother had believed, and maybe, given the time and the social mores of the community she'd lived in, that had been the only decision she could have made.

She remembered one of the few times her mother had talked of it. 'I was so frightened, so alone, and my parents were so, so thankful when Mike said he'd marry me. *I* was so thankful.'

And there it was, in a nutshell. Thankful. That gratitude thing.

Was it getting in the way of what she was feeling for Ben?

How could she know? Her emotions were so confused, a kaleidoscope of needs and wants. The way he'd held her hand had felt good, it had even felt right—but surely she was stronger than to let emotion influence her future? She would *not* let herself fall into this man's arms because she needed him.

But…she wanted him?

Yes, she did. She could admit that to herself. Ben was strong, kind, loyal. He was also…sex on legs?

You can cut that out, she told herself fiercely.

So…if you married him…

The need would come first, she told herself, and she knew it was true. Marriage had come up exactly twice now, once when he'd learned of the pregnancy, and today when he'd looked at his daughter on screen.

His daughter.

Unconsciously her hands went to her tummy and held.

'I will not let you be raised thinking your mother needs to be grateful to your father,' she said out loud. 'I will not! And it's his demons making him do the offering. Sweetheart, your relationship with your father is your business, and gratitude to him shouldn't come into that either. So he can take his offer of marriage and stick it.'

She gave a fierce nod and started dressing but dammit, here came the tears again. She swiped them away and hauled on her trousers with a ferocity that startled her. And then she swore because the zip broke.

Of all the…

'Well, that's what he can do while we wait for the return ferry,' she said, and she was still talking to the tiny baby she was carrying. A daughter! 'So the plan is that I'll sit in the cafeteria and hold my trousers together while your father goes out and buys me more. Stretchy ones. And I'll be grateful enough to pay for his coffee—even a doughnut! But that's as far as we should go. We can do this, us girls. We can cope.'

But they might well need his help.

So what, she told herself.

In the days after her mother's death, fighting a fog of depression and despair, she'd picked up a corny self help book. For some reason one of the lines resonated now.

Independence is there for the taking, but a smart women learns the art of accepting help with grace and courage.

Just after that appalling wedding day, a eucalypt had toppled over in her backyard and Anya had tried to clear it. She'd ended up covered with scratches but still with ninety percent of the tree untouched.

The next day she'd rung a neighbour. He'd arrived half an hour later with three mates, a truck, a mulcher and two chainsaws.

She'd hated that he wouldn't take payment, but he'd acted offended when she'd offered.

'Hey, Anya, we're friends, right?'

That night she'd fought an almost irresistible urge to cook him a tuna bake.

The memory made her smile, and the thought grounded her. She and Ben could be friends, and she *would* accept help from him.

But not marriage. That was payment far above the price she was prepared to pay.

Independence was gold.

He'd got it wrong again.

Ben sat in the cafeteria nursing a cooling mug of coffee and expected to feel regret, but this was much worse. This wash of anger, of grief, of helplessness was so strong it threatened to overwhelm him.

Of all the stupid, stupid, *stupid* things to say.

'Anya, please, we need to be married.'

He'd now proposed twice, and the memory of that first proposal was still with him.

'We'll have to get married.'

The look on Anya's face then was still seared in his memory.

And now…

'We need to be married.'

Same thing.

And it was wrong. Anya was a feisty, independent woman, with a career and a planned future. There was no need for a wedding ring.

So why had he blurted it out? Was that what he wanted? For Anya to need him?

He thought of Rihanna, false, manipulative, totally self-centred, and the difference couldn't be greater.

Was that why he wanted her? Because she was so different to Rihanna?

No. Over the last months they'd been a medical team for the island. He'd watched her work and been more than impressed with her skills. More, he'd been pretty much blown away with the relationships she was forming on the island.

She'd come to Dolphin like him, wanting a job where independence was everything, and to a certain extent that had happened. She did hold herself apart, yet there was never a time when she was less than generous with her patients, and less than caring.

And with the islanders themselves? She was getting to know the ins and outs of their lives. Off-duty, she'd be in the shallows happily playing with the island kids, or sitting on someone's porch happily gossiping, or…or just being happy.

She loved her life on the island. Her happiness was infectious too, and as he watched her, more and more he'd been hit by the urge to slough off the remnants of his past and join right in.

Was he falling in love with the island?

Or with Anya?

He was starting to know the answer.

Anya was taking her time—surely it didn't take this long to dress? Maybe she'd stopped to talk to the sonographer, maybe get a copy of the stills of their daughter.

Their daughter.

The idea was messing with his head. The echoes of Rihanna's two announced pregnancies were still with him, and both had left him with a weird sense of loss.

Was that why he wanted this baby so much?

What he wanted, suddenly but quite, quite desperately, was to wind back time. To meet Anya when they'd been med students, when they'd been free of every tie. Free of every ghost.

But Anya would still have had ties, obligations to Mathew and his community, obligations to the mother she'd loved.

He could have helped. He could have found some way of making things work for her.

So she'd be grateful to him rather than Mathew?

Dammit, this was doing his head in.

His leg cramped.

His physio had advised him: 'Whenever you can, choose standing over sitting. These cramps seem to be caused by pressure on your damaged spine, and keeping your spine stretched will help.'

Two hours on the ferry, a taxi ride to the hospital, another half hour's wait for the appointment and then sitting while he watched the ultrasound... What did he expect?

Pain?

He swore and rose and did a slow circuit of the cafeteria, wishing he still had his cane. It was pride that had made him leave it behind. He wanted to forget...

But he could never forget, and neither could Anya. Her rejection was based on self-protection—he knew that. And his proposal—what was that based on?

Her need? What kind of a basis was that for a proposal? So he'd stuffed it, but he didn't know how to make it right.

He thought of the times he saw her now on the beach, playing in the shallows with the island kids. He thought of her laughter, her empathy and her kindness.

He thought of that night on the river, feeding casseroles to the fish. Of her solitude and her pain.

This was so different to anything he'd felt before. It was a million miles away.

He managed two more circuits of the cafeteria before Anya appeared, looking self-conscious, tugging the hem of her shirt down to hide her hips. Her bump was clearly evident. She looked flustered but she was smiling.

That smile made his heart turn over.

But she wasn't into heart issues, and what should he expect after the stupid things he'd said to her?

'Problem,' she told him. 'Ben, I need your help.'

And that was good. Great even, because it put aside the tangled feelings that were doing his head in.

'Help?'

'My trousers have busted. Unless you want to take me home in my knickers, I need you to buy some more.'

'You're kidding.'

'Nope,' she said, and she grinned. 'I'm a maiden in distress and I need Sir Lancelot. Not for dragon-slaying, though—did Lancelot slay dragons? Regardless, I need a hero for something much more prosaic.'

He chuckled, thankful that the tension had eased. The cramps in his leg had eased as well. They sat while she checked online and located what she needed and then she sent Ben off in a taxi to fetch it.

See, I can help, he told himself ruefully as he left her in the cafeteria and headed off to find maternity trousers.

Just…not enough.

Not in the way he wanted.

CHAPTER TWELVE

WITH ANYA RESPECTABLE AGAIN, they headed back on the ferry. The incoming guests, a high-flying business group, headed for the cabin, quaffing champagne, already in party spirits.

That left Anya and Ben alone, on deckchairs in the bow of the boat.

They sat in near silence. It wasn't a bad silence, though. It was...peaceful.

That had been yet another dumb outburst of Ben's, Anya decided as the mainland disappeared in the distance and the outline of Dolphin Island grew closer. *'We need to be married.'* What a statement! She'd been furious, but time was giving her perspective. It had been the statement of someone who thought he owed her. Of a guy who was offering her the protection of his name.

It had made her feel angry and defensive and small—as if she couldn't cope by herself—but now, lying back in her deckchair, the sun on her face, she decided that it was his history with Rihanna, plus centuries of society norms that were making their marks.

If you made a girl pregnant you married her. Simple as that.

Like her parents.

Let it go, she told herself. She wasn't her mother. She had a great job, and she wouldn't be ostracised by having her daughter alone. The island was wonderful. She had great support.

And if Ben left?

Okay, that was a heart lurch, but only because he was a friend. There were lots of doctors out there who could fill his place.

Were there?

'Anya?' She was thinking but she was also dozing, letting the sun and the gentle motion of the water lull her to near sleep. But the thought of Ben leaving the island had jolted her and she was still aware of a gut lurch.

'Mmm?'

'What I said this afternoon…it was stupid.'

'So it was,' she said, peacefully enough.

'We don't need to be married.'

'No.' But she answered cautiously. Where was this going?

'I think, though,' he said, sounding as if each word was being considered, syllable by syllable, 'that I may just have fallen in love with you.'

She didn't open her eyes. *Caution!* her brain was screaming.

These words seemed a siren song—a gentle guy, a gorgeous, wounded hero, falling in love with her…

But there were two sets of words preceding this.

'We need to be married.'

'We'll have to get married.'

Was this more of the same? A more considered approach in his attempt to be honourable?

'That's nice.' She tried to make her words light, as if he'd just made a joke and she was responding in kind, but she knew her voice wobbled.

'Anya, I'm serious.'

Uh-oh. She needed to open her eyes. She needed to face this head-on.

'Ben, don't.'

'Don't speak the truth?'

'Don't spoil it,' she said, and the wobble was still there. 'We came here for a reason and that reason holds true. The fact that I'm having a baby shouldn't alter things.'

'The fact that we have a daughter…'

'It's important,' she agreed. 'But it should have nothing to do with the way we feel about each other.'

'So you don't think you could love me?'

She closed her eyes again, a defence, feeling as if a whole lot of balls had suddenly been thrown into the air and she was trying desperately to see

where they were. Which ones should she catch?
Which ones should she let go?

'Could we,' she said, very cautiously indeed,
'remove that entirely from the concept of marriage? I don't say I don't like you...'

'Wow, that's a start.'

Her eyes flew wide and she met his gaze. He
looked almost indignant. Suddenly she found
herself close to laughter. Guys, she thought. One
declaration that they might just be falling in love
and a woman was supposed to fall at his feet?
This was being held out to her like a candy bar.

I may just have fallen in love.

It was dumb, it was unfair, but the memory of
Mathew was still there.

*'We love each other, Anya, and it would make
more people than us happy. It makes sense to be
married.'*

Was this more of the same?

No. This man was a world apart from Mathew.
He was strong but gentle, skilled, kind, fun to be
with, a pleasure to work alongside.

And he had the loveliest eyes. His gaze held
hers and she felt herself begin to melt. What if...?

Get a grip!

'Not...not yet,' she managed. 'Ben, I can't. It's
way too soon. I keep seeing Mathew, my mum,
my parents' marriage. I need to prove to myself
that I don't need anyone. Does...does that make
sense?'

'Yes.' His look gentled. 'Yes, it does. Does me being around interfere with that?'

'No. Yes!' She shook her head. 'Ben, I don't know. All I do know is that I'm not ready for… for anything.'

'For being loved?'

'I don't know if I can love back.' She bit her lip, trying to make sense to herself. 'Ben, I like you, a lot, but you…you came along when I was in a mess and you brought me here. It was such an amazing thing to do, and what I feel for you now is all tied up with that.'

'You're saying you feel grateful?' Was there an edge of anger in those words? Regardless, they made her flinch.

'I don't know,' she said miserably. 'But I am thinking you rescued me.'

'You rescued yourself.'

'No.'

'You called off your marriage to Mathew all by yourself,' he said, gentle again. 'That took courage.'

'It did.' She tilted her chin. 'I should have done it years ago though, and here I am, drifting into another relationship.'

'We're not drifting,' he said, the edge back in his voice. 'What happened the night we created our daughter…was that drifting?'

'I guess…it was pretty near a full speed catastrophe.'

'Not a catastrophe,' he said, even more definitely, and he leaned over and took her hand in his. 'I think…a miracle. A miracle I'd like to share.'

'Well, you can share,' she said a trifle breathlessly. She felt so out of her depth here that she wasn't making sense even to herself. 'But that's our daughter's life we're talking about, not mine.'

'So there's no possibility…'

'Not…no,' she managed. 'This feels like cowardice but I… I can't.'

'But in time?'

'I don't know.' She tugged her hand free and stood up. As she did the ferry changed course into Dolphin Harbour. The direction of the swell changed abruptly and she staggered. Ben was on his feet in an instant, holding her, steadying her.

If felt right. It felt wonderful. She could sink into him, into his strength, into his promise of the future.

No. The boat steadied and so did she.

'Leave it, Ben,' she managed and pulled away. 'We're colleagues with a shared baby between us. Isn't that enough?'

'I guess…' He sighed. 'If that's the way you want it, then I guess it has to be.'

And then they were approaching the wharf. The staff team was there, waiting to take the incoming guests up to the resort, but oddly, Joe wasn't standing with them. He was out on the dock, waving as the ferry approached.

'Docs!'

'Uh-oh,' Ben said. 'What now?'

'We have a problem,' Joe called as the ferry slid into its berth. The gangplank hadn't been put in place yet and the resort guests hadn't emerged from the cabin. 'There's a stranding, a big one. Twenty or so dolphins out of water, around the headland past the research centre. No one goes there much so they could have been out of the water a while. It looks like they're dying.'

'Dying?'

'Yeah,' Joe said, looking gutted. 'Breaks your heart. The research team's there now and any resort staff we can spare as well. But you know what the research team is all about? Coral. If a lump of coral washed up they'd be our experts, but with dolphins they're just as useless as I am. And one of our guests has already been hit by a tail—Dorothy Vanson, would you believe? She and Henry have only just come back from the States, and they found them. They tried to pull one back to sea, somehow it hit her and she thinks she's broken her arm. Meanwhile Martin says he hasn't a clue about dolphins. He's radioed the mainland, but he can't find anyone to help, at least not until tomorrow, and he's already frantic about publicity. Twenty dead dolphins is what we don't need.'

He gestured to the door to the cabins. 'So…
With this new lot coming in I can't get away, and
even if I could, I dunno what the risks are. I can't
imagine you know any more about dolphins than
I do, but what's needed is someone with a bit of
authority. As medics, you're the best choice. Plus,
Dorothy needs attention and she and Henry are
refusing to come back to the resort until the dolphins are re-floated. As if that's going to happen fast. Docs, dead dolphins are one thing, but
the way things are going…you reckon you can
knock some order into things?'

'I'll go at once,' Ben said. 'But Anya…'

'Don't you dare put buts into this equation,'
she said before he could finish. 'I'm coming too.'

CHAPTER THIRTEEN

THE SCENE THAT greeted them as Ben steered the beach buggy over the sandhills was a gut lurch, to say the least.

Dolphin Island was the largest land mass of the Isles. Its west side was a sheltered coast-line that served to protect the brilliant corals of the Great Barrier Reef, but the cove Joe had directed them to was on the east, open to ocean swells. Large waves rolled in, running up the long stretch of wild beach.

And on the beach…dolphins. Ben pulled the buggy to a halt on top of the rise and they stared in dismay.

Assessment. Here was another edict drilled into them from med school. Don't rush in before you've gained the clearest idea possible of what you're facing.

What they faced seemed chaotic.

The wash of tide had created an almost la-goon type effect, a sandbank far out, with an inner pool of shallower water between sandbank and beach. At high tide the pool would have been deep enough to swim in, the sandbank low enough for dolphins to breach.

But the tide had obviously receded and left the creatures stranded. Their struggles had left them in an even worse situation. They were now lying on almost dry sand.

These were the animals they often saw from the beach near the resort, magnificent bottle-nosed dolphins, constantly leaping from the water in their hunt for the abundant fish around the isles, delighting all who saw them. These were the creatures who'd given the resort its name.

They were in deadly trouble.

But they did have help. A dozen or so people were trying desperately to keep them wet. They all seemed to have buckets and were ferrying them between the sea and the dolphins.

While Ben had been driving, Anya had been scrolling the internet on her phone, searching for information. Now she had a page that told her what they most needed.

'Point form,' she read out loud. 'First, stay clear of the tail, as it's strong and can cause injury. I guess that accounts for Dorothy's broken arm. Then keep them wet, covered with anything you can find, like towels or sheets, and bucket water on them. Apparently sunburn alone can kill them. But be careful not to pour water near their blow hole.'

'That'll be what they're doing,' Ben said, motioning to the helpers. 'But why on earth did they beach themselves?'

'It says here it often happens in a feeding frenzy. Mostly at high tide. Possibly they'll have been chasing a school of fish into the shallows. A big wave makes them think the water's deeper than it is, the wave's sucked out and they're stranded.'

Ben whistled in dismay. 'So what? Grab them by the tail and pull?'

'Definitely not,' she said, reading on. 'They're not used to pressure on their bellies, and it would cause damage. It says here, if possible, dig a trench around them and get water in. Even if it soaks in, the softer sand will help with the pressure. It says to dig holes under the side fins—the pectoral fins—so there's no pressure on them, either. If they're on their sides we need to dig a trench beside them and roll them back to their bellies. If they stay on their side the damage to their pectoral fins can be catastrophic.'

'But re-floating...' He was watching a couple of men already trying to pull a dolphin by the tail.

'We need to get down there,' Anya said urgently. 'The idea is to float them out, using mats or similar to manoeuvre them. But apparently they have to be re-floated all at once. Even when they're in the water, every animal needs to kept under control until we're sure they're stabilised. But if they're not released together there can be some sort of distress signal that'll cause released dolphins to re-strand.'

'Hell,' Ben muttered, staring down at the melee on the beach, then looking at the shallow water and the sandbank further out. 'So we're talking…next high tide…five or six hours?'

'Yep.'

'And all at once?'

'That's what it says.'

'We'll need an army.'

'I agree,' she said, looking down again at the information she was reading. 'It says here pretty much minimum four people per dolphin. Best bet is a sheet or tarp under them, then someone at each corner. Still protecting the fins, tucking them in, then moving them fast so pressure is kept to a minimum.'

'That means resort guests.'

'They'll come,' Anya said, and suddenly she found herself wincing, thinking of the champagne on the ferry. 'We might need to check for sobriety, but with six hours to go until high tide they have hours to sober up.'

'Will they come?'

'Um,' she said, still smiling. 'Isn't that a lesson that's been drilled into both of our heads? Nothing's more certain, people just love to help.'

Priority was people—it had to be. They headed down to the beach and found the Vansons, Dorothy and Henry. Since the day she'd helped out at the jet-ski accident, Anya had regarded Dorothy as a friend. The couple seemed to spend almost half the year at the resort, loving its climate, its gorgeous setting, the life away from what sounded a hectic social existence in the States.

But they didn't look social now. The usually flamboyant Dorothy was looking totally subdued, sitting on a rock, cradling her arm and staring out at the scene before her in dismay. Henry was clucking round her, looking worried.

'You can't do anything, dear, I'm sure it's broken.'

A quick glance between Anya and Ben, and Anya accepted her role.

She squatted beside them. As well as helping on that first day on the island, Henry needed constant reassurance that his blood pressure was stable. Dorothy had sliced her foot on a shell just before they'd headed back to the States and had needed treatment for an infected toe. Anya felt as if she knew them well, and she greeted them with a smile.

'Hey,' she said as Ben headed into the melee

of dolphins and helpers. 'Dorothy, you've hurt yourself.'

'We found them,' Dorothy told her, obviously fighting back tears. 'You know we just arrived back two days ago? We decided to re-explore the whole island, and when we got here the dolphins were just…here. So Henry took the buggy to the research centre for help and I stayed here. The water was deeper then, and I thought I might just try if I could pull one of the littler ones back into the sea. But I just managed to get a grip and… thwack. Oh, but these poor dolphins.'

'Let's get you back to the resort and fix you up,' Anya said. She was doing a visual assessment as she spoke. Dorothy's multicoloured kaftan had cut-out arms, allowing her a clear view of her lower arm. There was no obvious displacement, but the way she was cradling it, not touching it between wrist and elbow, told its own story.

'No!' She could hear the pain in Dorothy's voice, but also determination. 'If you could bind me up, dear, I'd be very grateful, but I want to stay here. If you tell him what to do then Henry can help, can't he? I know he wants to, and so do I. You can't tell us you have enough helpers.'

'We don't,' Anya agreed. 'But your arm…'

'It doesn't come before these creatures,' Henry said, nodding at Dorothy. 'I won't risk my wife's health, but if it's possible… These dolphins are a big part of the reason we come back here every year. They've given us such pleasure. Please, let us help.'

Hmm. 'Wiggle your fingers,' she told Dorothy, and she grimaced and then tried. She managed to move them though, just a fraction, but enough for reassurance that there was no nerve compression. On the surface, it looked like a simple fracture of the lower radius, not obviously displaced.

And behind her…

'I need your attention.' Ben's deep voice rang out over the beach, startling every helper, and Anya too. Probably even the dolphins. 'Everyone, listen up. If you're willing to keep helping, we thank you, but first priority is to protect yourselves. So absolute imperatives. One, avoid sunstroke. Doc Greer and I have a buggy full of supplies. I need two people—yep, you and you, to cart them down closer. We have plenty of sunscreen—help yourselves and reapply it often. Joe from the resort has loaded hats and a few long-sleeved shirts, so if you're not wearing them already, grab one. Also we have water bottles. Drink lots, often. I'll be checking as I come round and if I don't see empty water bottles I'll send you off the beach.'

'As for the dolphins, keep away from their beaks. They're feeling threatened already and they can bite. Also a swipe from their tail can do damage. These animals need help but if you're ill yourself you'll take resources we can use for them.'

Beside her Dorothy winced, but Anya touched her good arm. 'Hey, don't beat yourself up,' she told her. 'You and Henry got the help these guys need, so well done.'

'Next, care and control of dolphins lesson one,' Ben was booming. 'These guys can't be floated until high tide—that's what the experts tell us. They also need to be released all at once, or we risk them re-stranding. We have a long wait. It'll be dark before they can be released, so if you're willing to help we need to focus on keeping them safe until then. We need to stop them getting sunburned. We need to keep them wet, avoid damage to their fins and we need to take the pressure off their bellies...'

And as she listened Anya could almost feel the surge of communal relief. Someone knew what to do. Someone was in charge.

Meanwhile her priority was Dorothy.

'I'm not going back to the resort,' Dorothy repeated. 'If you can tie me up so I don't do any more damage... What's a broken arm?'

Anya winced but Henry grinned and reached out and patted his wife's cheek. 'That's my girl.' He glanced up at Anya and gave her a firm nod. 'So that's the decision. We're tough.'

'Yeah?' Neither of them looked tough. They were both in their eighties. Henry looked like a retired businessman on vacation—wearing a polo with a golfing club insignia, Bermuda shorts, a shock of white hair and an air of authority. Dorothy was wearing a gorgeous silk kaftan, her silvery-white curls were beautifully bouffant and...were they real pearls around her neck? Regardless, they both looked equally determined.

'Dorothy and I have been through a lot,' Henry was saying. 'We've lost a baby. Our second daughter was born deaf. Dorothy's been through breast cancer. We've been through a business collapse...'

'Oh, and our house burned down when the children were tiny,' Dorothy added, as if it was just a minor inconvenience. 'We're both tough.'

'But I'm not into dolphin care until my Dorothy's fixed,' Henry added. 'We'll take no stupid risks. If you say we have to go back to the resort then we won't fight you, but we both go. No matter what, we do things together.'

'You lost a baby?' Anya said faintly, and Dorothy gave a nod she was starting to realise was characteristic of them both.

'Yes, we did. She lived for just three days. We've had three more since, and now we have five grandchildren. They call us Mops and Pops. Our friends say that's ridiculous, but we think they're the best names in the world. Even so, after all this time, our Miriam's still a hole in our hearts.'

And then she checked. 'Oh, my dear! You're pregnant! I hadn't realised. I'm so sorry—you shouldn't think of such things.'

'My baby's fine,' Anya said, and realised she sounded defensive, but there was no way she could be anything else. 'I...we had a scan this morning. She's perfect.'

'*We* had a scan?' Dorothy's intelligent face brightened with interest.

'Dr Duncan came with me,' she said without thinking. And then, for some reason she didn't understand herself, she found herself adding, 'Ben... Dr Duncan...he's the baby's father.'

Why had she said it? It was the first time she'd admitted it to anyone but, for some reason, at this moment it felt right. And Dorothy beamed, her broken arm seemingly forgotten.

'Oh, that's lovely! He was so good to us when I had that toe infection. To have someone like that beside you...'

'He'll be great,' she agreed, feeling confused. This wasn't the way most patient/doctor consultations went. 'I... I'm very grateful.'

And Dorothy's beam disappeared, almost as if she'd been slapped.

'Grateful?'

'To have his support, I mean,' she said, too fast. 'Now, let's see to that arm.'

But both Henry and Dorothy were staring at her as if she'd said something obscene. 'Grateful?' Henry said in tones of disbelief.

'I guess… I didn't mean that.'

'But you think it?'

She hesitated and then said honestly, 'He will support us both,' she told them. 'I try not to think it's a cause for gratitude, though. I know he doesn't want me to.'

'I should think not!'

Somehow she recalibrated. Where was this conversation going? 'Enough,' she said, trying to sound brisk, competent—in charge. 'We have twenty or so dolphins needing our help. Let's get you into the buggy. I'll take you over to the research centre, where I can check that arm properly. Personal stuff can come later.'

'Yes, dear,' Dorothy said as Henry helped her up by holding her good arm. 'And I know it's none of our business, but it's not irrelevant. It can't be. Surely gratitude has no place when you love someone.'

'We don't love each other.'

'No?' Dorothy said dubiously, and glanced across the beach to where Ben was helping lay towels over a dolphin's gleaming back. 'Why not?'

'Because…'

'Because it's none of our business,' Dorothy repeated. 'We get it. But dear, you can't possibly fall in love with someone you're grateful to. It wouldn't work. Why not put that aside?'

'Who said I needed to fall in love?'

'Well, if I were you I would. He's lovely.'

'Hey,' Henry interjected, and Dorothy almost managed a giggle.

'Well, he is. It's just lucky I met you first,' she said demurely as they started walking, a little unsteadily, up the sandhill to their parked buggy. 'And I'm so grateful that I did,' she told her husband. 'But that's the end of gratitude. You and I, love, we've been through the hoops and we're now…well, we're just… Mops and Pops. Us. Gratitude turned into something much, much deeper a very long time ago.'

'And you…' She turned and smiled at Anya, a gentle, considering smile that encompassed not only Anya but also her nicely rounding bump.

'If Dr Duncan is father to your child, if he wants to be a part of your life… Dear, I know I don't have all the details, and Henry'll give me heaps later for putting my nose where it has no business…but…well, he's gorgeous and he *is* part of your life, like it or not. So I surely don't know what you need, but if I were you I'd stop thinking about being grateful and start thinking how to get him into my bed and keeping him there.'

'Dorothy!' Henry said, startled. 'For heaven's

sake! She's an incurable matchmaker,' he told Anya. 'Ignore her. For all Dorothy knows, he might have three wives already.'

'I guess,' Dorothy said reluctantly. 'But if he hasn't…'

'Um,' Anya managed. 'Moving on, people. Let's…'

'Move on,' Dorothy repeated. 'Yes, dear, but if he doesn't have three wives…' She sounded almost wistful. 'You know, our second daughter almost missed out on a perfectly lovely relationship because she had qualms. She's deaf, you see, and she thought he was just being kind. It took so long to convince her to go for it, and now she's so happy. And Dr Duncan… He's just… beautiful! But you're right. Enough of matchmaking. Let's fix my arm and go save some dolphins.'

Anya was starting to feeling totally discombobulated. What she needed was to retreat to medicine, and fast.

The research centre was only a few hundred metres around the headland, and she could use their facilities to check Dorothy's arm. She led the couple to one of the buggies, but as she helped Dorothy climb in, she couldn't help glancing back at the beach. Those who hadn't applied sunscreen were busy doing so. Those who had were already starting to dig sand out from under pectoral fins.

Chaos was already starting to look like teamwork.

Ben was… beautiful?

Cut it out, she told herself, but her thoughts refused to be cut.

They had to be cut! What was she doing, thinking that Ben in control mode seemed like sex on legs?

It was not helpful, she told herself. It was not helpful at all, and there was work to do.

Ideally she'd have sent Dorothy straight to the mainland, for X-ray and the immediate care of an orthopaedic surgeon. With their money, transport by chopper was surely possible, as was care by the best of Queensland's medical specialists.

But the couple was adamant they were staying until the dolphins were released, so she settled Dorothy in the director's office and examined the arm with more attention than she'd been able to give on the beach.

She had movement—painful but still possible—in her fingers. There was no numbness, which meant no nerve damage, and the arm was still in alignment. The tail had slapped down hard over her extended arm. She could feel a slight distension and the arm was swelling already. But with movement, with feeling, with the fact that tenderness was at the wrist but not at the elbow, she decided her initial tentative diagnosis of a fractured lower radius was probably right.

'You'll need to go to the mainland to get it X-rayed and set properly,' she told her. 'But I can fix it with a makeshift back slab to hold it firm and bind it tight against your chest. If you promise not to try and move it, I can give you enough painkillers so it can wait until morning.'

'I promise,' Dorothy said. 'But let's do it fast. I want to see what's happening on the beach.'

'You know high tide's not for hours. It'll be a long wait.'

'I can scoop trenches with one hand,' Dorothy said. 'And Henry can use both. There's no way we're leaving now, right, love?'

'No way at all,' Henry agreed.

'Some people—our children included,' Dorothy said darkly, 'think eighty-year-olds should be tucked into bed at nine with a cup of cocoa and a hot-water bottle. Saving dolphins…how cool is this?'

'As long as we can,' Henry said warningly. 'Love, some of them might not make it.'

'Not on our watch,' Dorothy declared. 'Let's get this arm bound and get back to it.'

CHAPTER FOURTEEN

WHAT FOLLOWED WAS five gruelling hours where Ben and Anya's skills as medics were needed almost as much as the skills required to keep the dolphins alive.

Back at the resort, Martin had moved into organisational mode. Within an hour of news of the dolphin stranding, social media had alerted mainstream news outlets. The Dolphin Isles were a source of fascination to the world in general, dolphins were a heart tug, and by dusk a media chopper was hovering over the beach, its lighting flooding the scene. Height had to be maintained in order to stop sand blowing or the noise scaring the dolphins further, but its light was a huge advantage.

As was the influx of guests from the resort. As soon as the news filtered through, guests were volunteering en masse, but Martin was still smarting from the impact on the resort from the drunken jet-ski accident. He thus did a fast and ruthless cull. Volunteers had to be not only fit but able to swim and also able to pass a breath test. Security was sent to block the access track to anyone else.

Martin had also been onto the mainland, requesting veterinary assistance, and both Ben and Anya were updated by phone.

'Check on each animal before release,' the chief veterinarian at a mainland sea mammal rehabilitation centre told them. 'A wounded dolphin can't be released—often its struggles will cause the whole pod to re-strand. Given the urgency of re-floating and the impossibility of getting any wounded animal away from the pod, it's better to euthanise.'

So as the hours wore on, as the tide inched its way back in, Anya and Ben found themselves medically checking each dolphin. It had to be a cursory assessment. Weights, blood tests, internal problems were impossible to assess in this time frame, but the vet gave them enough information to make a best guess.

'They should have included dolphin training in our university course,' Anya complained to Ben. 'They won't cough or stick out their tongues when I tell them to.'

'Inconsiderate critters,' Ben said. They'd been working from one side of the beach to the other and had finally met in the middle, but the work had taken hours.

Each dolphin had been assigned four volunteers, who were continuously wetting the animal's skin or scooping the underlying sand, imperative to stop pressure building. Even more important than assessing the animals, Anya and Ben had also been asking questions of these volunteers, making a best guess of fitness, assigning roles accordingly.

At least four people would be needed to carry each dolphin into the water, and once there, according to the vet's advice, each dolphin would have to be held and gently rocked for at least thirty minutes so they could stabilise. Martin had sent over wetsuits from the resort's water sports supply, the research centre also had heaps, but wetsuits weren't the only need.

As the hours passed, Anya and Ben needed to watch for exhaustion, for any signs that people were working past their limits. Any volunteers who'd managed to get past Martin's fitness assessment had to be gently told they needed to stay ashore.

'And that's not in my skill set either,' Anya complained to Ben. 'I just told Dorothy she'd absolutely need to stay onshore and she almost hit me.'

'She and Henry were the ones to sound the alarm so maybe they should get to give the release signal,' Ben suggested, smiling.

They were both feeling relieved. Even though their dolphin examinations had been necessarily limited, neither of them had found any sign of major injury. The vet had told them that some strandings were caused by an ill and disoriented member of the pod, but these all looked sleek and fit.

'And schools of tuna have been cruising around the headland over the last week,' one of the research team had told them. 'I'd imagine these guys were undone by greed, nothing else.'

So yay, healthy dolphins. They had enough volunteers and enough wetsuits. They'd thought about using sheets to carry the dolphins into the water, but Ben had discarded the idea—too flimsy. Dorothy had come up with a solution. 'Those gorgeous quilts that are on all the beds back at the resort…'

Martin's response to the idea was horror, but…

'That chopper up there's taking pictures,' Henry said, his businessman mode coming to the fore. 'Resort staff carrying dolphins out to sea on magnificent resort-coloured quilts… Tell the man that's publicity gold.'

And a dazed Martin had agreed. The quilts had arrived, had been tested for grip quality, had been approved and were lying ready to slide under the dolphins as the water rose. It was now just a matter of waiting.

'So…you?' Ben asked. He'd been gazing out over the floodlit beach but now he turned to

Anya and his gaze gentled. 'You must be exhausted.'

'I'm tired but I'm okay.'

'I can cope if you need to go home to bed.'

'Are you kidding?' Their position as medics had seen them assume an automatic role of authority, and no one else seemed remotely able to share. Yes, she was tired, but leaving…

'You can't carry,' he told her. 'Or stay in the water.'

'I know that.' She'd accepted it reluctantly. Some concessions had to be made to her pregnancy and a thump from a dolphin's tail could be a disaster. 'Though I reckon I could still get into a wetsuit.'

'Beer belly, pregnancy bump, what's the difference?' he teased, and she chuckled and gave his arm a thump.

'Thanks. But you shouldn't go in either. You know your leg's still weak.'

'I'd imagine I'm one of the strongest swimmers here, though. Try and stop me.'

'Ever the hero. Your role obviously extends past replacing a maiden's busted pants.'

'Too right it does,' he said and grinned, and then silence fell. They stood looking out over the sea of dolphins and helpers, at the floodlit beach, at the sight of so many doing whatever they could—and then Ben looked down into her face and his smile changed. 'Anya, I would so much like that role to extend.'

'Ben…'

'Yeah, not the time,' he said, and fell silent again.

It was a weird time, a hiatus of peace. Checking had been done. Roles had been assigned. Volunteers were now deepening trenches beside each animal. The idea was that as soon as the waves reached them the quilts could be manoeuvred under.

But for the two of them it was now just a matter of waiting. Of being on call if needed. Of standing in the weird light cast by the chopper, or the moonlight when the chopper disappeared—to refuel, to swap machines, who knew? Of watching the waves slowly inching up the beach.

And for Anya…to feel this sensation within grow and grow.

They weren't touching. They were simply standing side by side, and yet it felt as if they were closer. There was some intangible link that seemed to be growing stronger by the minute.

And his words seemed to be echoing.

'Anya, I would so much like that role to extend.'

She knew what he meant.

He'd made two clumsy proposals of marriage. She'd rejected them both and she'd been right to do so. Both had been made at times when emotions were high, the first when they'd discovered she was pregnant, the second when they'd properly seen their daughter. Those proposals had felt like nothing to do with her.

And yet, standing beside him now, the feeling grew stronger that there was far more below the surface of those two awkward declarations.

A hero would have made those first two declarations, she thought. A knight in shining armour, declaring that he would marry his pregnant woman. A hero, looking at the image of his daughter and swearing he would give her a family.

But she stood beside him and she thought, *No. He's no hero. He's just... Ben.*

She was suddenly remembering another night, of Ben wading into the rippling shallows of the river at Merriwood, of his smiles, his understanding. She was thinking of his empathy that first night on the island, disregarding the shallowness of the dumb Mia and guessing the threat of violence beneath the surface. She was thinking of the pain she saw etched on his face when he'd done a hard workout, of the determination he was showing to recover completely.

To recover from the trauma of a disastrous marriage. To recover from betrayal and injury and loss.

She suddenly felt very, very small. This man

had asked her to marry him and she'd reacted…
with anger.

The chopper swept away into the night—to
refuel again? They'd know release wouldn't be
until high tide, almost an hour away. She imagined they'd be back then, ready to broadcast dra-
matic images to the nation.

If this went right, the publicity for the resort
would be awesome. Guests helping to save dolphins. It'd be headline news.

But behind the scenes… She looked across the
beach at the huddle of people working by every
single dolphin. To the world tomorrow they'd be
the resort's wealthy guests, millionaire businessmen and women, actors, politicians, the world's
Who's Who. But tonight they were just…here.
Doing their best.

She glanced along the beach to where Dorothy
and Henry were back, sitting on the rock where
she'd first seen them. They'd both been scooping
sand, but she'd sent them for an enforced break,
insisting they drank the coffee Martin had sent
over and then rested until the time came for release.

Martin had also sent over blankets—lots of
them—so they were now wrapped in cashmere,
huddled tight together.

And Dorothy's words were suddenly replaying in her head?

'But, dear, you can't possibly fall in love with

*someone you're grateful to. It wouldn't work.
Why not put that aside?'*

What if she put gratitude aside? What if she
was seeing this man for the first time, meeting
him casually, dating with no strings, having a
second date, a third? Not getting pregnant. No
baggage.

And then…she'd be standing here in the
moonlight and she'd be doing…what?

Moving closer. Of course she would.

And she was hearing Dorothy's words again
when she'd declared, *'We don't love each other.'*

Dorothy had said, *'Why not?'*

Why not indeed? The question was suddenly
almost exploding in her head.

But then it settled, as if panic had somehow
been averted. And she was thinking, I haven't
blown it. He's still here.

Ben.

And before she could second-guess herself she
moved, just a little, so her arm ever so slightly
brushed his.

And she lifted his hand into hers and held.

For a moment there was nothing. No reaction
at all. It was as if her movement had left them
both frozen.

Had she blown it? Panic swept through her.
Had she messed with her chances?

The moment stretched on, but still she held.
Held his hand. Held her breath.

And then, very slowly, as if caution had to be maintained every inch of the way, his fingers curved around hers, interlinked and held. Strongly, surely, certainly.

He turned and looked down into her face and she looked up at him. Maybe she smiled.

Ben didn't smile. He simply looked into her eyes and what he saw there she didn't know.

Maybe it was a reflection of what her heart was screaming. *Please. Oh, please.*

And then, very gently, his other hand came up and cupped her face. It was a feather touch, so soft, so tender it made her want to weep.

'Anya,' he said, and he needed to say no more. There was such a depth of meaning…

It was okay. No, it was…

She couldn't think. There were no words.

'Hey,' she managed, because she couldn't think of anything else to say, and even the word *hey* was stupid. There was nothing that fitted this moment.

Maybe they needed…nothing.

The moment stretched on. They didn't kiss. They stayed still and silent, the wash of the incoming tide, the moonlight on their faces, the background murmur of the volunteers on the beach, all fading to nothing.

They simply had each other.

And then a wave swept in, bigger than those that had come before. The incoming tide had meant that the pools of water in the trenches beside the dolphins had been filling of their own accord, but this wave swept through the trenches, even managing to slightly lift some of the dolphins closest to the sea.

'It's time to get those quilts under,' Ben said but his voice was unsteady and his eyes hadn't left hers.

'Yes, it is.'

'So it's time for a happy-ever-after for our dolphins,' he said, and then, 'Anya, what about us?'

'We might see,' she said, cautiously, but with slivers of joy suddenly seeming to light her world. 'But…but let's not think of ever after. Let's maybe think about cautious, tentative beginnings.'

And then the events of the night took over. After that first wave, others followed, surging up the beach, around the dolphins. The tide, however, must have been higher when they'd stranded or maybe—more likely, as these creatures were known for their intelligence—it had been a freak wave that had swept them in. Because as the point of high tide was reached, they were still in a mere six inches of water.

It was enough, though. Each dolphin had had a quilt manoeuvred carefully under its belly, with loops tied at the corner. One of the hotel guests had volunteered that he'd been a Queen's Scout, and he'd personally organised the impressive and, he swore, dependable hand holds.

So as the dolphins felt the water surge around them, as their instinct had them wanting to thrash, the volunteers took up their positions.

They worked under Ben's orders. Each step of the way he was in control.

Anya quietly walked among the groups, silently observing. Watching for any sign of strain among the volunteers, any hint that such a weight might be too much, that no one was disguising or risking injury in their desire to be part of this rescue.

'We're about to move,' Ben told them. 'We'll wait for a decent surge and then we go together. Straight into the water, as fast as you can, over the sandbank and then to chest depth of the smallest person of your party. No deeper. Then we hold. One person, the strongest of the group—work it out now, people—controls the peduncle...'

He was getting his instructions via an earpiece from the mainland vet, and he decided explanation was necessary. 'The peduncle's the base, the stalk if you like, of the tail. If it's loose it'll thrash it and make the dolphin impossible to hold. So one person, the strongest of you, holds that. The rest of you need to apply weight to the upper body, but still keeping that blowhole as clear as you can. Then you need to rock from side to side, allowing your dolphin to get used to the water. We need to make sure they can self-right if rolled to the side, and that they can surface to breathe unassisted.'

'Why can't we just let them go?' someone called.

'Because we don't want them to re-strand,' Ben called back. 'Our vet says we need to sta-bilise them for at least thirty minutes, because if one's in trouble they all might be. We keep them as close together as we can, then, on my signal, we release. We make sure the quilt has dropped away—someone from each group can gather it back. Then, on my word, we step be-hind and form a human chain between them and the beach. We slap the water, kick, yell, make as much commotion as possible, so the clear way for any disoriented dolphin is out to sea. Any questions?'

There were none.

'And the moment any of you are unsure of your footing, feeling unwell, feeling anything other than completely in control, then you get out of there. Dr Greer will be on the beach ready to help. There's no way we'll tell the world tomor-row that we rescued twenty dolphins and lost one investment banker.'

'Now there's a choice,' someone called, and there was general laughter, and then another wave swept in.

Ben called, 'Any time now'. The scene was set.

And it worked.

Anya stayed on the beach with the small group of volunteers who'd self-declared the rescue was beyond their capability. Dorothy and Henry were among them. Dorothy was clutching Henry's hand as if she were drowning and whenever Anya was in range Henry took hers.

This couple were no longer patients. They were friends.

Anya was trying to watch all her little beach tribe. These were people Martin had passed as fit to help but some of them were elderly, they'd been working for hours and they should be showing signs of strain. But without exception they were so entranced by the scene before them that health issues were forgotten.

It was Anya's job to watch their faces and assess, but even Dorothy, pumped full of painkillers, looked far too excited to be worrying about a mere broken arm.

She did have one patient. A woman in her forties, Prue, left her dolphin and stumped to shore in a filthy mood. 'I've cut my foot on a shell,' she glowered. 'Dr Duncan says bleeding can attract sharks or I'd stay. Stupid foot. Can you wrap it up tight, Doc, so I can still watch?'

Anya complied, but with one eye still on the water. It was a rough bandage—she'd have to clean and rewrap later—but there was no way either of them would miss what was about to happen.

Blessedly the moon was full, playing over the disparate group in the water, twenty dolphins and the helpers working to get their dolphins stabilised.

But there were no problems. This might look like a motley band of onlookers, but under Ben's calm directions they became a well drilled army.

Overhead the chopper had returned. It hovered almost motionless, lighting the scene. The waves were washing almost shoulder height, the backs of the dolphins shining in the combined beam of floodlight and moonlight, and the whole world seemed to hold its breath.

And then, finally, on Ben's signal, the order was called by Dorothy in a tone that'd do a sergeant major proud. Ben had planned to repeat it, but there was no need.

'Release!'

There was a moment more of stillness as each dolphin realised they were no longer held. And then…organised chaos. Each volunteer—including those who'd stayed on the beach—now rushed to be part of this final glorious moment.

Within seconds they'd formed the most riotous human chain they could manage, banging on the water, yelling, waving their arms, forming a barrier between the dolphins and the beach they'd just left.

And finally, almost as one, the realisation of freedom dawned and the dolphins moved out, into the oncoming waves.

There followed the holding of breath by every person on the beach... *Please*...

And then the pod became a unit, a glorious, leaping surge of gleaming dolphins, glimmering outward through the moonlit waves. They disappeared, plunged down, under again and then up, out, further and further. Not one dolphin faltering. Not one dolphin lost.

And people were laughing, crying, cheering, watching until they were out of sight and then wading through the shallows to hug everyone they could find. Henry and Dorothy—by now everyone knew who'd found them and raised the alarm—were raised on shoulders and whooped in what was almost a tribal dance of celebration. Retirees, businessmen and women, nerdy scientists who spent their lives studying the drift of coral spawn... They were all one.

And then somehow Anya was plucked from the midst of the crowd, scooped up in two very wet arms—clad in wetsuit rubber—and held and twirled and held and held and hugged and held and kissed.

The noise on the beach seemed to die away. Had Ben carried her away from the crowd or was it just that there was no room in her heart for the crowd to exist?

Regardless, she was held against his chest, her weight apparently nothing. *His leg*, the doctor in her should have screamed. *His back. What are you doing? Are you out of your mind?*

But right now she was no longer a doctor. She was no longer anything but a woman who was deeply intent on returning a kiss she seemed to have been waiting for all her life.

Ben's kiss.

Her kiss.

This was a kiss of love. A kiss of commitment. A kiss with the promise of a future she knew now was inevitably hers.

And when she finally surfaced she found they had an audience. The crowd had come back into focus. The dolphins had finally leapt and glimmered and disappeared, so now, instead of watching the dolphins finally reach their freedom, almost every person on the beach was watching a man kiss a woman. As if it was part of the same promise. The same magic of this night.

She should mind. She should be embarrassed.

She should fight to be put down. She should…
do nothing.

Nothing else mattered.

Nothing else at all.

'I love you,' Ben whispered when there was
finally room for the whisper of words between
them.

'Then that's perfect,' she managed before kiss-
ing him again. 'Because I believe I love you right
back.'

It was past three in the morning before Anya and
Ben could make it to bed. Ben had practically
ordered Anya to leave him to it, but she'd seen
the way he'd limped up the beach to the buggies
and she was having none of it.

There was still work to be done. They were
risking nothing—every volunteer had to be in-
dividually checked. There were scrapes, bruises,
strains. The morning would see this motley crew
aching from unaccustomed exertion, and it was
Anya and Ben's job to see that there'd be nothing worse.

They cleaned grazes, they stitched the two
cuts—one guy hadn't realised he'd cut himself
until he stripped off his wetsuit and he still wasn't
sure what had happened. They'd fixed Dorothy's
arm more securely, had given her painkillers to
last the night and had organised a chopper to take
her to the mainland in the morning.

They could have organised it now, but Dorothy was having none of it. 'If you think a mere broken arm will stop me sleeping then think again. What a glorious night,' she'd said as the couple had left the makeshift clinic that Martin had organised in Reception. 'Perfect.' One armed, she still managed to hug Ben but she hugged Anya the hardest. 'Oh, my dear, I'm so happy for you.'

And then at last they were done, free to find their own beds. They walked silently along the dimly lit path to Anya's studio—that was the closest. And then they paused.

On the doorstep was a tray. A tiny porcelain casserole and a Thermos.

A note was attached.

Dolphin Isles Resort thanks you for the contribution you've made to tonight's outstanding rescue. Microwave three minutes on high.

'Yay,' Anya said a trifle unsteadily. She was linked to Ben, hand holding hand, and she was starting to feel so tired that she might topple if she let go. 'I hadn't even realised I was hungry.'

'Bless the kitchen staff,' Ben said. 'What's the betting there's one at my place too.' There was a moment's hesitation and then his grip on her hand tightened. 'Anya, what about we pick this up, take it over to my place and put them together?'

And for the first time that night his voice was unsteady. Unsure? She looked up into his face and saw a question.

He still didn't know. She had to say.

And somehow she did. 'Yes,' she said, and then she tilted her face to kiss him. 'Yes, and yes, and yes.'

And he smiled, and all the joy of the night—no, maybe all the joy in the world was in that smile. He scooped up the casserole and took her hand again.

'Don't you need your cane?' she asked suddenly, the thought only just occurring to her. The strain on his injured leg tonight must have been enormous, and she hadn't seen the cane all night.

'I'm done with it,' he said and tugged her closer as they turned to the path to his bungalow. 'You can hold me up when I need it.'

It was enough to make her heart sing. They walked in silence, the emotions of the night almost too much for words.

An identical tray was waiting on Ben's doorstep. They carried it inside and set it on the table.

They were covered in salt and sand. They needed showers. They desperately needed—and desperately wanted—bed. That glorious king-sized bed that was probably still split in two. They could push it together again and...

'But I'm really hungry,' Ben said, sounding apologetic, and as if in reply Anya's stomach gave a low but unmistakable growl. They wanted to make love, right there, right then, but the need for food was suddenly even greater.

'So what do we have?' Ben said, and lifted the casserole lid and sniffed. And then his face broke into silent laughter as he lifted it to let her do the same. 'Anya...'

She sniffed and her eyes widened. 'Tuna bake,' she said faintly, and they stared at each other, their faces creasing into disbelieving laughter.

'Do we...do we feed this to the fish?' Ben asked at last, as laughter finally eased.

'Don't you dare,' she managed and marched her casserole to the microwave. 'We're going to eat these together—and, what's more, we're going to be very, very grateful.'

CHAPTER FIFTEEN

THE DAY WAS GLORIOUS. The island was sun-drenched, the palms were creating dappled shade over the beach and the soft breeze was creating the merest ripple on the glistening ocean.

There'd been a school of whiting darting through the shallows earlier this morning. A pod of dolphins had eaten their fill and was now cruising lazily out past the waves, occasionally surfacing, seemingly content to drift and maybe even watch the goings-on on the beach.

Who knew what they'd make of what was happening? But dolphins were the most intelligent of mammals. Maybe they could even make sense of it.

They could likely see the cluster of humans, surely different creatures than the wetsuit-clad saviours who'd tugged them to safety six months before. These humans were dressed in the bright-est of colours, flowing sarongs, colourful shirts, bare feet, drifts of frangipani tucked into hair or around necks, great garlands of frangipani strung over an arch where a man and a woman stood holding hands.

No. Holding one hand each. The woman— could dolphins differentiate between the sexes?— was using her free hand to cradle…

A young. A bundle of soft white and pink.

Young dolphins were born much larger than this. How did they survive? a dolphin might have wondered. Put that one in the water and see how it went.

But it didn't seem to be worrying the pair under the arch. They looked as if all was right in their world.

As one, the pod of dolphins rode in on the next wave—maybe to take a decent look? Then they cruised out through the breakers, twisting and leaping and heading back out to sea.

Enough. The humans might be happy, but breakfast was obviously done. Now, what about lunch?

And on the beach…

Vows.

'I, Anya Louise Greer, take you, Benjamin James Duncan…'

'I, Benjamin James Duncan, take you, Anya Louise Greer…'

This wedding was right. It was perfect. It was their day, their glorious affirmation of what was deep inside them both.

It wasn't the grand society wedding Ben's parents would have liked, although they were here too, besotted with their tiny granddaughter and learning to love Anya on her own terms.

Nor was it a formal wedding where everyone who'd ever been good to them had had to be invited. Janet and Beth were here from Merriwood, but they'd mutually decided that Mathew and Jeanie could be left off the guest list.

Because this was simply a gathering of those who they knew wished them joy.

That included all the islanders, the research staff and the resort staff. Martin had warned incoming guests on booking that on this day service would be minimal.

'You're worth it,' he'd told them.

The filming of the dolphin rescue had been broadcast pretty much internationally. It seemed the corporate guests had been the top echelons of a breathtakingly powerful conglomerate. They'd shared their experience far and wide, and there were consequentially no gaps in the resort's booking for years.

There were, though, places still reserved for 'permanent' guests. Dorothy and Henry had flown back to the States a month after the 'night of the dolphins', but they'd returned before the birth of Aisha Reyna Duncan. And when Anya had gone into labour three weeks before her due date, when the birth had been hard and fast, when there'd been no time to get to the mainland, Dorothy had restated her ex-nurse status. She'd thus acted as midwife as Ben had delivered their precious baby girl.

'Henry and I feel almost like we have another grandbaby,' she'd told Anya the next morning. 'Can we be Mops and Pops again? Oh, my dear, what a wonderful extra reason for spending half our lives here.' She was blinking back tears. 'And do you know, she looks a tiny bit like our Miriam.'

The birth had been perfect, Anya thought mistily as she made her vows. As everything was perfect. This place, this life, this man.

Ben. She loved him with all her heart. He was making his vows now, and the joy in her heart was overwhelming.

They'd stay here, they'd decided. Why not? What had started as an interim step, a place for them both to recover until they could face the world again, had become, quite simply, their world.

The resort was growing—as was the research station. The publicity surrounding the dolphin rescue had prompted voices calling for a marine rescue centre to service the outer islands. Ben had been at the forefront, studying marine veterinary care online, making trips to the mainland to learn more. Anya intended to join right in.

They'd be doctors, vets—and friends.

Best friends, she thought, as Ben slipped a

ring onto her finger, and she gazed into his eyes and saw her own deep love reflected straight back at her.

Friends, lovers, partners.

In her arms Aisha gave a tiny squirm and a mew that might have been one of utter contentment. Their little girl surely knew enough not to complain on this day, the beginning of a life that promised so much.

'Our family,' Ben murmured. They looked down into their daughter's perfect little face and then, of one accord, they kissed. It was a sandwich hug, with their baby cradled between them, and there was a collective sigh from the crowd around them.

'You know what?' Ben said when finally they drew apart and there was room again for words between them. 'I'm grateful.'

'Well, how about that?' Anya managed. 'I'm grateful too. But not...not *to* you, Ben Duncan. I'm grateful *for* you.'

'Ditto, my Anya,' he said softly and tugged her close again. 'For you, for our daughter, for this, our happy ever after. And for...life.'

* * * * *